THE STORY OF LITTLE DOMBEY

AND OTHER PERFORMANCE FICTIONS

THE STORY OF LITTLE DOMBEY

AND OTHER PERFORMANCE FICTIONS

Charles Dickens

a *Broadview Anthology of British Literature* edition

broadview press

Library and Archives Canada Cataloguing in Publication

Dickens, Charles, 1812-1870
    The story of little Dombey and other performance fictions
/ Charles Dickens ; general editors, Joseph Black ... [et al.].

(Broadview anthology of British literature)
Includes bibliographical references.
ISBN 978-1-55481-164-9

    1. England—Social life and customs—19th century—Literary collections. 2. Recitations. I. Black, Joseph, 1962- II. Title.
III. Series: Broadview anthology of British literature

PR4553.B63 2013   823'.8   C2013-900200-6

Broadview Press is an independent, international publishing house, incorporated in 1985.

We welcome comments and suggestions regarding any aspect of our publications—please feel free to contact us at the addresses below or at broadview@broadviewpress.com.

North America	PO Box 1243, Peterborough, Ontario, Canada K9J 7H5
	2215 Kenmore Ave., Buffalo, New York, USA 14207
	Tel: (705) 743-8990; Fax: (705) 743-8353
	email: customerservice@broadviewpress.com
UK, Europe, Central Asia,	Eurospan Group, 3 Henrietta St., London WC2E 8LU, UK
Middle East, Africa, India,	Tel: 44 (0) 1767 604972; Fax: 44 (0) 1767 601640
and Southeast Asia	email: eurospan@turpin-distribution.com
Australia and New Zealand	NewSouth Books, c/o TL Distribution
	15-23 Helles Ave., Moorebank, NSW, Australia 2170
	Tel: (02) 8778 9999; Fax: (02) 8778 9944
	email: orders@tldistribution.com.au

www.broadviewpress.com

Developmental Editors: Don LePan and Laura Buzzard

Broadview Press acknowledges the financial support of the Government of Canada through the Canada Book Fund for our publishing activities.

This book is printed on paper containing 100% post-consumer fibre.

PRINTED IN CANADA

Contents

Introduction • 7
    Performance Fictions • 11
    A Note on the Text • 13

The Story of Little Dombey • 15
Mrs. Gamp • 41
David Copperfield • 51
Sikes and Nancy • 87

In Context: The Readings of Charles Dickens • 103
    From Novel to Performance Fiction • 103
        from Charles Dickens, *Dombey and Son* (1846–48) • 104
        from Charles Dickens, "The Story of Little Dombey" (1858) • 105
    Reviews • 107
        "Mr. Charles Dickens's Readings," *The Era* (13 June 1858) • 107
        from "Mr. Charles Dickens's Readings," *The Belfast News-Letter*
            (30 August 1858) • 109
        from "Charles Dickens in Derby," *The Derby Mercury* (27 October
            1858) • 111
        "Mr. Charles Dickens," *The Times* (8 January 1859) • 113
        from "Mr. Dickens's First Reading," *The New York Times*
            (10 December 1867) • 115
        from "Mr. Dickens as a Reader," *The New York Times* (16 December
            1867) • 119
        Mark Twain, "Charles Dickens," *The Alta California* (5 February
            1868) • 122
    Descriptions • 125
        from Kate Field, *Pen Photographs of Charles Dickens's Readings*
            (1868) • 125
        from Charles Kent, *Charles Dickens as a Reader* (1872) • 127

Introduction

Few English novelists have attracted the huge audiences and lasting fame of Charles Dickens. People the world over are familiar with the moral transformation of *A Christmas Carol*'s Ebenezer Scrooge and the life of the orphan Oliver Twist, immortalized in his piteous request for a second bowl of water gruel: "Please, sir, I want some more." From Pickwick and Sam Weller in *The Pickwick Papers* to Mr. Micawber in *David Copperfield* to Pip in *Great Expectations*, from Mr. Guppy and Mrs. Jellyby in *Bleak House* to Mr. Gradgrind in *Hard Times* and Flora Finching in *Little Dorrit*, Dickens created a panoply of memorable characters. Combining comic genius with astute criticism of the laws and institutions of Victorian society, he created novels that continue to command the attention of critics and the general public alike.

Dickens's early childhood was signally important as source material for the concerns and themes of his novels. His father worked as a naval office clerk in Portsmouth when Charles was born in 1812, the second of 10 children (two died in infancy). John and Elizabeth Dickens aspired to a middle-class life, but had unending difficulties controlling their spending and were always on the brink of penury. At one time, they served a four-month stint in the Marshalsea debtors' prison. Charles was able to attend school in Chatham, near London, after the family was transferred to the dockyards there, but in 1823 his education was halted, and he joined his parents in Camden Town, London. The young Dickens worked at odd jobs for his parents and was eventually sent off to work at Warren's Boot Blacking Factory at the age of 12. The psychological impact of this environment on Dickens was permanent; he never forgot the humiliation he had suffered or the dismay he had felt at the relatively harsh working conditions under which he and other children were forced to toil.

After the family came into a modest inheritance, Dickens returned to school, but in 1827, at just 15 years of age, he left school again because his father was unable to pay the fees. Working as a clerk in a law firm, he studied shorthand in his spare time, eventually becoming a parliamentary reporter. In 1833, *Monthly Magazine* published Dickens's first story, "A Dinner at Poplar Walk." While working as a newspaper reporter the next year, he launched a highly popular series of articles that were eventually collected and published as *Sketches by Boz* (his journalistic pseudonym) in 1836. The success of the sketches led to another series that cemented his fame and secured his financial stability (thereby also allowing him to marry Catherine Hogarth, to whom he had become engaged in 1835). A monthly illustrated serial about the Pickwick Club was commissioned by publishers Chapman and Hall, and the absurd characters of Mr. Pickwick, Mr. Winkle, Mr. Tupman, Mr. Snodgrass, and Sam Weller soon had people all over England clamoring for the latest installment of *The Pickwick Papers*. Dickens consolidated this success by beginning *Oliver Twist* (1837–38) in *Bentley's Miscellany*, which he had begun editing, and then launching *Nicholas Nickleby* (1838–39) as a monthly serial.

In 1837, Dickens and his wife began to raise a family (they eventually had 10 children). In this same year, he lost his beloved sister-in-law, Mary Hogarth, who would become the inspiration for Little Nell in *The Old Curiosity Shop* (1840–41) and for many of the childlike women that constitute the "good angels" of his novels. By the time this book was published, Dickens's fame had spread throughout North America; eager fans would line the piers in New York waiting for the latest installment of a Dickens story to arrive from England.

In 1842, Dickens journeyed to the United States to take advantage of his fame, but the trip turned out to be a disappointment. He was put off by the hordes that crowded around him relentlessly, trying to speak to, touch, or even just glimpse the famous author. He scorned, publicly and at any opportunity, the lack of international copyright laws (Americans could pirate editions of his books without any of the proceeds going to him). He set out his disdain for American habits (such as chewing and spitting tobacco) and for American institutions, such as slavery and what he thought was a ruthless prison system, in a book about his travels, *American Notes* (1842), and made Americans the object of derision in his novel *Martin Chuzzlewit* (1843–44). Not surprisingly, the American press reacted with an outpouring of vindictive editorials. (As it happened, *Martin Chuzzlewit* did not sell well on either side of the Atlantic.) Americans began to forgive Dickens after the appearance in 1843 of the overwhelmingly successful *A Christmas Carol*, (1843), the first in his Christmas book series and a work of fiction strongly focused on the virtues of forgiveness and generosity of spirit.

Dickens was astonishingly energetic. From 1850 onwards he edited the weekly magazine *Household Words* (for which he wrote many of the pieces himself); he wrote and acted in theatrical works; he traveled widely; he worked on behalf of various social causes—and he continued to produce major novels at a steady pace. *Dombey and Son* (1846–48) was followed by *David Copperfield* (his most autobiographical work, 1849–50), *Bleak House* (1852–53), *Hard Times* (1854), *Little Dorrit* (1855–57), *A Tale of Two Cities* (1859), *Great Expectations* (1861), and *Our Mutual Friend* (1865).

Dickens published all of his novels in serial form. The episodic structure of his novels prompted him to develop methods of characterization that allowed immediate identification of characters by readers waiting for weekly or monthly installments. He also developed an extraordinary talent for weaving together numerous strands of story material and coincidental events that, however implausible they might appear, somehow strike the reader as persuasive. This approach to story and to characterization has proved to be an ongoing source of fascination for critics. In Dickens's own day George Eliot lamented what she perceived to be its defects almost as strongly as she lavished praise on what she felt to be its strengths:

> We have one great novelist who is gifted with the utmost power of rendering the external traits of our town population; and if he could give us their psychological character—their conceptions of life, and their emotions—with the same truth as their idiom and manners, his books would be the greatest contribution Art has ever made to the awakening of social sympathies.

In the early twentieth century the novelist E.M. Forster famously drew on the example of Dickens in defining the terms "flat" and "round" characters:

> Dickens' people are nearly all flat.... Nearly every one can be summed up in a sentence, and yet there is this wonderful feeling of human depth. Probably the immense vitality of Dickens

causes his characters to vibrate a little, so that they borrow his life and appear to lead one of their own. It is a conjuring trick....

At the dawn of the twenty-first century the critic James Wood, in suggesting that Dickens has been "the overwhelming influence" on British fiction since World War II, extended Forster's analysis:

> Many of Dickens's characters are, as Forster rightly put it, flat but vibrating very fast.... Their vitality is a histrionic one.... One obvious reason for the popularity of Dickens among contemporary novelists is that Dickens's world seems to be populated by vital simplicities.... Dickens licenses the cartoonish, coats it in the surreal.... Yet that is not all there is in Dickens, which is why most contemporary novelists are only his morganatic heirs. There is in Dickens also an immediate access to strong feeling, which rips the puppetry of his people, breaks their casings, and lets us enter them.

The "immediate access to strong feeling" that Dickens's fictions provided was certainly a central part of their appeal in the Victorian era. The story of "Little Dombey" is a case in point. From its first appearance in serialized form in January 1847, the episode of *Dombey and Son* in which Paul Dombey dies (at the end of the fifth installment) has been acknowledged as one of Dickens's most powerful. Dickens's friend John Forster described it as having sparked nothing less than "national mourning" when it first appeared; the novelist William Thackeray is reported to have declared excitedly after he had read it that it was impossible to compete with "such power as this.... [The] chapter describing young Paul's death is unsurpassed—it is stupendous." Together with the death of Little Nell in *The Old Curiosity Shop*, it was the strongest example of Dickens's ability to move his Victorian readers.

In 1858 Dickens separated from Catherine; the break was complicated by his relationship with the actress Ellen Ternan and by the degree of publicity that (partly at Dickens's instigation) attended his change in marital status. In that same year, Dickens began an extensive series of public readings, a lucrative but exhausting enterprise that severely compromised his health. He continued touring throughout the 1860s while editing his new journal, *All the Year Round* (begun in 1859). Dickens was at work on *The Mystery of Edwin Drood* when he died in 1870 during a grueling schedule of readings. In his will Dickens requested that he be buried at Rochester, Kent, near his home. Under public pressure the family agreed to allow him to be buried instead in Poet's Corner in Westminster Abbey. Dickens's instructions that the funeral be "unostentatious, and strictly private" were followed, however; there were only a dozen present for the ceremony in the cathedral.

Performance Fictions

In the 1830s and 1840s it began to be common for literary societies, Mechanics' Institutes, and other groups to sponsor public lectures, recitals and one-man performances; many who considered the stage immoral began to be drawn to readings of, for example, scenes from Shakespeare staged in public halls. In 1846 the idea came to Dickens of holding public readings of his own work: "I was thinking the other day," he wrote to his friend John Forster, "that in these days of lecturings and readings, a great deal of money might possibly be made … by one's having readings of one's own books. I think it would take immensely." Forster discouraged the idea, and Dickens did not put it into practice immediately. It was not until more than a decade later, after William Thackeray had begun to enjoy great success with audiences, that Dickens decided to present readings of his own work. The two took very different approaches; according to one nineteenth-century account, Thackeray "read so as to be perfectly heard, and perfectly understood, and so that the innate beauty of his literary style might have full effect." Dickens, who was an accomplished amateur actor, is described by a contemporary as having "read quite differently. He read not as a writer to whom style is everything, but as an actor throwing himself into the world he wished to bring before his hearers."

Dickens became almost as famous for his readings as he was for his novels; particularly memorable was his triumphal tour of America in 1867–68, in which he earned what would in today's money be several million dollars for 76 performances. (In New York alone, some 40,000 people are estimated to have attended his readings.)

Dickens shaped his fictions for presentation, trimming and revising material from his novels and stories to create readings that would be self-contained artistic entities. In the case of "The Story of Little Dombey" he took as his raw material Chapters 1, 5, 8, 11, 12, 14, and 16 of his novel *Dombey and Son*, cut out story material that he felt was extraneous or would not work well as part of a public performance, and eliminated several minor characters. (The character of Toots, however, he expanded somewhat.) The conclusion of the story of Paul Dombey was already famous as being among the most emotionally affecting moments in all of Dickens's novels, and the readings made it more famous still; during his first provincial tour Dickens reported that "The Story of Little Dombey" was his "greatest triumph everywhere." (It was somewhat less well received in America.)

The reading Dickens created from his novel *Martin Chuzzlewit* combines scenes featuring the widely beloved character of Sarah Gamp. Dickens never ceased making alterations to his performance texts, and this one was no exception; the first reading of "Mrs. Gamp" was based on material from Chapters 19 and 25 of the novel, but a major revision omitted much of the original ending and added a new one drawn from Chapter 49. Integrated with these plot points were some of the choicest Cockney comments and mangled quotations for which the character was so well known. Critical opinion regarding Dickens's performance of this piece was sharply divided; it was praised as "the most comic of all the readings" but also derided as "a miserable imitation of two old women using *low English slang*."

Extracting a reading from *David Copperfield* proved to be a much greater challenge than *Martin Chuzzlewit* or *Dombey and Son*. As Dickens wrote in 1855,

> I have been poring over Copperfield (which is my favourite), with the idea of getting a reading out of it.... But there is still the huge difficulty that I constructed the whole with immense pains, and have so woven it up and blended it together that I cannot yet so separate the parts as to tell the story of David's married life with Dora, and the story of Mr. Peggotty's search for his Niece, within the time.

He made several attempts at the task until, finally, in 1861 he succeeded in creating a 120-page script, which he would go on to reduce by more than a third. Critics and audiences appreciated the results of his efforts—especially the harrowing account of the storm with which the reading concludes—and, as Dickens observed, his performance "positively enthralled the people."

"Sikes and Nancy" is a condensation of some of the most dramatic events in *Oliver Twist*; the material is a substantially re-written version of Chapters 47, 48, and 50 of the novel. Dickens was initially afraid of how audiences on his reading tour would react to the violent content, so he tried it out on a hundred guests at a special reading first. His audience was captivated, and it became a regular in his repertoire. Dickens threw himself into the performance of all his readings, but none more so than "Sikes and Nancy." "I shall tear myself to pieces," he is reported to have said as he was about to go onstage to perform this reading for what turned out to be the final time, on 8 March, 1870.

A Note on the Text

Most of Dickens's readings were published during his lifetime, first individually and then together as *The Readings of Mr. Charles Dickens, as Condensed by Himself* (1868); "The Story of Little Dombey," "Mrs. Gamp," and "David Copperfield" are based on the texts that appeared in this collection. "Sikes and Nancy" had not yet been performed when *The Readings of Mr. Charles Dickens* was published, and so of course was not included; the text of that reading is based on a version that Dickens had printed privately. The dates given at the end of each reading are of its first performance, but the texts incorporate any revisions Dickens made up to the time of printing. Spelling and punctuation have been modernized.

For those wishing to explore further the manner of Dickens's performances, *Charles Dickens: The Public Readings* (1975), edited by Phillip Collins, is an invaluable resource; it contains a wealth of information on each text, and includes transcriptions annotated to show the underlinings and other guides to performance that Dickens provided for himself in his prompt copies.

The Story of Little Dombey

Rich Mr. Dombey sat in the corner of his wife's darkened bedchamber in the great arm-chair by the bedside, and rich Mr. Dombey's Son lay tucked up warm in a little basket, carefully placed on a low settee in front of the fire and close to it, as if his constitution were analogous to that of a muffin, and it was essential to toast him brown while he was very new.

Rich Mr. Dombey was about eight-and-forty years of age. Rich Mr. Dombey's Son, about eight-and-forty minutes. Mr. Dombey was rather bald, rather red, and rather stern and pompous. Mr. Dombey's son was very bald, and very red, and rather crushed and spotty in his general effect, as yet.

Mr. Dombey, exulting in the long-looked-for event, the birth of a son, jingled his heavy gold watch-chain as he sat in his blue coat and bright buttons by the side of the bed, and said:

"Our house of business will once again be not only in name but in fact Dombey and Son; Dom-bey and Son! He will be christened Paul, of course. His father's name, Mrs. Dombey, and his grandfather's! I wish his grandfather were alive this day!" And again he said, "Dombey and Son."

Those three words conveyed the one idea of Mr. Dombey's life. The earth was made for Dombey and Son to trade in, and the sun and moon were made to give them light. Common abbreviations took new meanings in his eyes, and had sole reference to them. A.D. had no concern with anno Domini, but stood for anno Dombei—and Son.

He had been married ten years, and, until this present day on which he sat jingling his gold watch-chain in the great armchair by the side of the bed, had had no issue.[1]

—To speak of. There had been a girl some six years before, and she, who had stolen into the chamber unobserved, was now crouching in

---

[1] *issue* Children.

a corner whence she could see her mother's face. But what was a girl to Dombey and Son!

Mr. Dombey's cup of satisfaction was so full, however, that he said: "Florence, you may go and look at your pretty brother, if you like. Don't touch him!"

Next moment, the sick lady had opened her eyes and seen the little girl; and the little girl had run towards her; and, standing on tiptoe, to hide her face in her embrace, had clung about her with a desperate affection very much at variance with her years. The lady herself seemed to faint.

"Oh Lord bless me!" said Mr. Dombey, "I don't like the look of this. A very ill-advised and feverish proceeding having this child here. I had better ask the Doctor if he'll have the goodness to step up stairs again"; which he did, returning with the Doctor himself, and closely followed by his sister Mrs. Chick, a lady rather past the middle age than otherwise, but dressed in a very juvenile manner, who flung her arms round his neck, and said—

"My dear Paul! This last child is quite a Dombey! He's such a perfect Dombey!"

"Well, well! I think he *is* like the family. But what is this they have told me, since the child was born, about Fanny herself. How is Fanny?"

"My dear Paul, there's nothing whatever wrong with Fanny. Take my word, nothing whatever. There is exhaustion, certainly, but nothing like what I underwent myself either with George or Frederick. An effort is necessary. That's all. Ah! if dear Fanny were a Dombey! But I dare say, although she is not a born Dombey herself, she'll make an effort; I have no doubt she'll make an effort. Knowing it to be required of her, as a duty, of course she'll make an effort. And that effort she must be encouraged, and really, if necessary, urged to make. Now, my dear Paul, come close to her with me."

The lady lay immoveable upon her bed, clasping her little daughter to her breast. The girl clung close about her, with the same intensity as before, and never raised her head, or moved her soft cheek from her mother's face, or looked on those who stood around, or spoke, or moved, or shed a tear.

There was such a solemn stillness round the bed, and the Doctor seemed to look on the impassive form with so much compassion and so little hope, that Mrs. Chick was for the moment diverted from her purpose. But presently summoning courage, and what she called presence of mind, she sat down by the bedside, and said in the tone of one who endeavours to awaken a sleeper,

"Fanny! Fanny!"

There was no sound in answer but the loud ticking of Mr. Dombey's watch and the Doctor's watch, which seemed in the silence to be running a race.

"Fanny, my dear, here's Mr. Dombey come to see you. Won't you speak to him? They want to lay your little boy in bed—the baby, Fanny, you know; you have hardly seen him yet, I think—but they can't till you rouse yourself a little. Don't you think it's time you roused yourself a little? Eh?"

No word or sound in answer. Mr. Dombey's watch and the Doctor's watch seemed to be racing faster.

"Now really, Fanny my dear, I shall have to be quite cross with you if you don't rouse yourself. It's necessary for you to make an effort, and perhaps a very great and painful effort, which you are not disposed to make; but this is a world of effort, you know, Fanny, and we must never yield when so much depends upon us. Come! Try! I must really scold you if you don't. Fanny! Only look at me; only open your eyes to show me that you hear and understand me; will you? Good Heaven, gentlemen, what is to be done?"

The physician, stooping down, whispered in the little girl's ear. Not having understood the purport of his whisper, the little creature turned her deep dark eyes towards him.

The whisper was repeated.

"Mamma!"

The little voice, familiar and dearly loved, awakened some show of consciousness, even at that ebb. For a moment, the closed eyelids trembled, and the nostril quivered, and the faintest shadow of a smile was seen.

"Mamma! Oh dear mamma! Oh dear mamma!"

The Doctor gently brushed the scattered ringlets of the child aside from the face and mouth of the mother. And thus, clinging fast to that frail spar within her arms, the mother drifted out upon the dark and unknown sea that rolls round all the world.

We must all be weaned. After that sharp season in Little Dombey's life had come and gone, it began to seem as if no vigilance or care could make him a thriving boy. In his steeple-chase towards manhood, he found it very rough riding. Every tooth was a break-neck fence, and every pimple in the measles a stone wall to him. He was down in every fit of the whooping-cough. Some bird of prey got into his throat, instead of the thrush; and the very chickens, turning ferocious—if they have anything to do with that infant malady to which they lend their name—worried him like tiger-cats.

He grew to be nearly five years old. A pretty little fellow; but with something wan and wistful in his small face, that gave occasion to many significant shakes of his nurse's head. She said he was too old-fashioned.

He was childish and sportive enough at times, but he had a strange, weird, thoughtful way, at other times, of sitting brooding in his miniature armchair, when he looked (and talked) like one of those terrible little Beings in the Fairy tales, who, at a hundred and fifty or two hundred years of age, fantastically represent the children for whom they have been substituted. At no time did he fall into this mood so surely as when—his little chair being carried down into his father's room—he sat there with him after dinner, by the fire.

On one of these occasions, when they had both been perfectly quiet for a long time, and Mr. Dombey only knew that the child was awake by occasionally glancing at his eye, where the bright fire was sparkling like a jewel, little Paul broke silence thus:

"Papa! what's money?"

Mr. Dombey was in a difficulty; for he would have liked to give him some explanation involving the terms "circulating-medium, currency, depreciation of currency, paper, bullion, rates of exchange, value of precious metals in the market," and so forth; but looking down at the little chair, and seeing what a long way down it was, he answered:

"Gold, and silver, and copper. Guineas, shillings, half-pence. You know what they are?"

"Oh yes, I know what they are. I don't mean that, papa; I mean, what's money after all?"

"What is money after all!"

"I mean, papa, what can it do?"

"You'll know better by and by, my man. Money, Paul, can do anything."

"It isn't cruel, is it?"

"No, a good thing can't be cruel."

"As you are so rich, if money can do anything, and isn't cruel, I wonder it didn't save me my mamma. It can't make me strong and quite well, either. I am so tired sometimes, and my bones ache so, that I don't know what to do!"

Mr. Dombey became uneasy about this odd child, and, in consequence of his uneasiness, resolved to send him, accompanied by his sister Florence and a nurse, to board with one Mrs. Pipchin at Brighton—an old lady who had acquired an immense reputation as "a great manager" of children; and the secret of whose management was, to give them everything that they didn't like and nothing that they did.

Mrs. Pipchin had also founded great fame on being a widow lady whose husband had broken his heart in pumping water out of some Peruvian mines. This was a great recommendation to Mr. Dombey, for it had a rich sound. Broke his heart of the Peruvian mines, mused Mr. Dombey. Well! a very respectable way of doing it.

This celebrated Mrs. Pipchin was a marvellous ill-favoured, ill-conditioned old lady, of a stooping figure, with a mottled face, like bad marble, a hook nose, and a hard grey eye, that looked as if it might have been hammered at on an anvil. Forty years at least had elapsed since the Peruvian mines had been the death of Mr. Pipchin; but his relict still wore black bombazeen.[1] And she was such a bitter old lady that one was tempted to believe there had been some mistake in the application of the Peruvian machinery, and that all her waters of gladness and milk of human kindness had been pumped out dry, instead of the mines.

The castle of this ogress was in a steep by-street at Brighton; where the small front gardens had the unaccountable property of producing nothing but marigolds, whatever was sown in them; and where snails were constantly discovered holding on to the street doors, and

---

1 *black bombazeen* Material made of silk and worsted and commonly worn in mourning.

other public places they were not expected to ornament, with the tenacity of cupping-glasses. There were two other very small boarders in the house when Little Dombey (first called so by Mrs. Pipchin) arrived. These were one Master Bitherstone, from India, and a certain Miss Pankey. As to Master Bitherstone, he objected so much to the Pipchinian system, that before Little Dombey had been established in the house five minutes he privately asked that young gentleman if he could give him any idea of the way back to Bengal. As to Miss Pankey, *she* was disabled from offering any remark by being in solitary confinement for the offence of having sniffed three times in the presence of visitors. At one o'clock there was dinner, and then this young person (a mild little blue-eyed morsel of a child, who was shampooed every morning, and seemed in danger of being rubbed away altogether) was led in from captivity by the ogress herself, and instructed that nobody who sniffed before visitors ever went to heaven. When this great truth had been thoroughly impressed upon her, she was regaled with rice, while all the rest had cold pork, except Mrs. Pipchin, whose constitution required warm nourishment, and who had hot mutton-chops, which smelt uncommonly nice. Also, at tea, that good lady's constitution demanded hot toast, while all the rest had bread and butter.

After breakfast next morning Master Bitherstone read aloud to the rest a pedigree from Genesis (judiciously selected by Mrs. Pipchin), getting over the names with the ease and clearness of a young gentleman tumbling up the treadmill. That done, Miss Pankey was borne away to be shampooed; and Master Bitherstone to have something else done to him with salt water, from which he always returned very blue and dejected. Then there were lessons. It being a part of Mrs. Pipchin's system not to encourage a child's mind to develop itself like a young flower, but to open it by force like an oyster, the moral of all her lessons was of a violent and stunning character; the hero—always a naughty boy—seldom, in the mildest catastrophe, being finished off by anything less than a lion or a bear.

At the exemplary Pipchin, Little Dombey would sit staring in his little arm-chair by the fire, for any length of time.

Once she asked him, when they were alone, what he was thinking about.

"You," said Paul, without the least reserve.

"And what are you thinking about me?"

"I have been thinking you ain't like my sister. There's nobody like my sister."

"Well! there's nobody like me, either, perhaps."

"Ain't there though? I am very glad there's nobody like you!"

"Upon my word, sir! And what else are you thinking about me?"

"I am thinking how old you must be."

"You mustn't say such things as that, young gentleman. That'll never do."

"Why not?"

"Never you mind, sir. Remember the story of the little boy that was gored to death by a mad bull for asking questions."

"If the bull was mad, how did he know that the boy had asked questions? Nobody can go and whisper secrets to a mad bull. I don't believe that story."

"You don't believe it, sir?"

"No."

"Not if it should happen to have been a tame bull, you little Infidel?"

As Paul had not considered the subject in that light, and had founded his conclusions on the alleged lunacy of the bull, he allowed himself to be put down for the present. But he sat turning it over in his mind, with such an obvious intention of fixing Mrs. Pipchin presently, that even that hardy old lady deemed it prudent to retreat.

Such was life at Mrs. Pipchin's; and Mrs. Pipchin said, and they all said, that Little Dombey (who watched it all from his little arm-chair by the fire), was an old, old fashioned child.

But as Little Dombey was no stronger at the expiration of weeks of this life than he had been on his first arrival, a little carriage was got for him, in which he could lie at his ease, with an alphabet and other elementary works of reference, and be wheeled down to the seaside. Consistent in his odd tastes, the child set aside a ruddy-faced lad who was proposed as the drawer of this carriage and selected instead a weazen,[1] old, crab-faced man, who was the lad's grandfather.

With this notable attendant to pull him along, and Florence always walking by his side, he went down to the margin of the ocean every

---

1 *weazen* Wizened.

day; and there he would sit or lie in his carriage for hours together, never so distressed as by the company of children—his sister Florence alone excepted always.

"Go away if you please," he would say to any child who came to bear him company. "Thank you, but I don't want you."

Some small voice, near his ear, would ask him how he was, perhaps.

"I am very well, I thank you. But you had better go and play, if you please."

Then he would turn his head and watch the child away, and would say to Florence, "We don't want any others, do we? Kiss me, Floy."

He had even a dislike, at such times, to the company of his nurse, and was well pleased when she strolled away, as she generally did, to pick up shells and acquaintances. His favourite spot was quite a lonely one, far away from most loungers; and with Florence sitting by his side at work,[1] or reading to him, or talking to him, and the wind blowing on his face, and the water coming up among the wheels of his bed, he wanted nothing more.

"Floy," he said one day, "where's India, where the friends of that boy Bitherstone live—the other boy who stays with us at Mrs. Pipchin's?"

"Oh, it's a long, long distance off."

"Weeks off?"

"Yes, dear. Many weeks' journey, night and day."

"If you were in India, Floy, I should—what is it that Mamma did? I forget."

"Love me?"

"No, no. Don't I love you now, Floy? What is it?—Died. If you were in India, I should die, Floy."

She hurriedly put her work aside, and laid her head down on his pillow, caressing him. And so would she, she said, if he were there. He would be better soon.

"Oh, I am a great deal better now! I don't mean that. I mean that I should die of being so sorry and so lonely, Floy!"

Another time, in the same place, he fell asleep, and slept quietly for a long time. Awakening suddenly, he listened, started up, and sat listening.

Florence asked him what he thought he heard.

---

1 *work* Needlework.

"I want to know what it says. The sea, Floy—what is it that it keeps on saying?"

She told him that it was only the noise of the rolling waves.

"Yes, yes. But I know that they are always saying something. Always the same thing. What place is over there?" He rose up, looking eagerly at the horizon.

She told him that there was another country opposite, but he said he didn't mean that; he meant farther away—farther away!

Very often afterwards, in the midst of their talk, he would break off, to try to understand what it was that the waves were always saying; and would rise up in his couch to look towards that invisible region, far away.

3

At length Mr. Dombey, one Saturday, when he came down to Brighton to see Paul, who was then six years old, resolved to make a change, and enrol him as a small student under Doctor Blimber.

Whenever a young gentleman was taken in hand by Doctor Blimber, he might consider himself sure of a pretty tight squeeze. The Doctor only undertook the charge of ten young gentlemen, but he had always ready a supply of learning for a hundred, and it was at once the business and delight of his life to gorge the unhappy ten with it.

In fact, Doctor Blimber's establishment was a great hot-house, in which there was a forcing apparatus incessantly at work. All the boys blew[1] before their time. Mental green-peas were produced at Christmas, and intellectual asparagus all the year round. No matter what a young gentleman was intended to bear, Doctor Blimber made him bear to pattern, somehow or other.

This was all very pleasant and ingenious, but the system of forcing was attended with its usual disadvantages. There was not the right taste about the premature productions, and they didn't keep well. Moreover, one young gentleman, with a swollen nose and an excessively large head (the oldest of the ten who had "gone through" everything), suddenly left off blowing one day, and remained in the

---

1   *blew* Flowered; bloomed.

establishment a mere stalk. And people did say that the Doctor had rather overdone it with young Toots, and that when he began to have whiskers he left off having brains.

The Doctor was a portly gentleman in a suit of black, with strings at his knees, and stockings below them. He had a bald head, highly polished; a deep voice; and a chin so very double, that it was a wonder how he ever managed to shave into the creases.

His daughter, Miss Blimber, although a slim and graceful maid, did no soft violence to the gravity of the Doctor's house. There was no light nonsense about Miss Blimber. She kept her hair short and crisp, and wore spectacles, and she was dry and sandy with working in the graves of deceased languages. None of your live languages for Miss Blimber. They must be dead—stone dead—and then Miss Blimber dug them up like a Ghoul.

Mrs. Blimber, her mamma, was not learned herself, but she pretended to be, and that did quite as well. She said at evening parties, that, if she could have known Cicero, she thought she could have died contented.

As to Mr. Feeder, B.A., Dr. Blimber's assistant, he was a kind of human barrel-organ, with a little list of tunes at which he was continually working, over and over again, without any variation.

To Dr. Blimber's Paul was taken by his father, on an appointed day. The Doctor was sitting in his portentous study, with a globe at each knee, books all round him, Homer over the door, and Minerva[1] on the mantelshelf. "And how do you do, Sir," he said to Mr. Dombey, "and how is my little friend?" When the Doctor left off, the great clock in the hall seemed (to Paul at least) to take him up, and to go on saying, over and over again, "how, is, my, lit, tle, friend, how, is, my, lit, tle, friend."

"Mr. Dombey," said Doctor Blimber, "you would wish my little friend to acquire—"

"Everything, if you please, Doctor."

"Yes," said the Doctor, who, with his half-shut eyes, seemed to survey Paul with the sort of interest that might attach to some choice little animal he was going to stuff—"yes, exactly. Ha! We shall impart a

---

1   *Homer* Ancient Greek poet; author of the *Iliad* and the *Odyssey; Minerva* Classical goddess of wisdom.

great variety of information to our little friend, and bring him quickly forward, I dare say. Permit me. Allow me to present Mrs. Blimber and my daughter Cornelia, who will be associated with the domestic life of our young Pilgrim to Parnassus.[1]

"Who is that at the Door? Oh! Come in, Toots; come in. Mr. Dombey, sir. Our head boy, Mr. Dombey."

The Doctor might have called him their head and shoulders boy, for he was at least that much taller than any of the rest. He blushed very red at finding himself among strangers, and chuckled aloud.

"An addition to our little portico, Toots; Mr. Dombey's son."

Young Toots blushed again; and finding, from a solemn silence which prevailed, that he was expected to say something, said to Paul, with surprising suddenness, "How are you?" This he did in a voice so deep, and a manner so sheepish, that, if a lamb had roared, it couldn't have been more surprising.

"Take him round the house, Cornelia," said the Doctor, when Mr. Dombey was gone, "take him round the house, Cornelia, and familiarize him with his new sphere. Go with that young lady, Dombey." So Cornelia took him to the schoolroom, where there were eight young gentlemen in various stages of mental prostration, all very hard at work, and very grave indeed. Toots, as an old hand, had a desk to himself in one corner; and a magnificent man, of immense age, he looked, in Little Dombey's young eyes, behind it. He now had license to pursue his own course of study, and it was chiefly to write long letters to himself from persons of distinction, addressed "P. Toots Esquire, Brighton, Sussex," and to preserve them in his desk with great care.

Young Toots said, with heavy good nature—

"Sit down, Dombey."

"Thank you, sir."

Little Dombey's endeavouring to hoist himself on to a very high window-seat, and his slipping down again, appeared to prepare Toots's mind for the reception of a discovery.

"I say, you know, you're a very small chap."

"Yes, sir, I'm small. Thank you, sir."

---

1 *Parnassus* Mountain in Greece associated with the Muses, goddesses of classical mythology who inspire learning and the arts.

For, Toots had lifted him into the seat, and done it kindly, too.

"Who's your tailor?" inquired Toots, after looking at him for some moments.

"It's a woman that has made my clothes as yet. My sister's dressmaker."

"My tailor's Burgess and Co. Fash'nable. But very dear."[1]

Paul had wit enough to shake his head, as if he would have said it was easy to see *that*.

"I say! It's of no consequence, you know, but your father's regularly rich, ain't he?"

"Yes, sir. He's Dombey and Son."

"And which?"

"And Son, sir."

Mr. Toots made one or two attempts to fix the firm in his mind; but, not quite succeeding, said he would get Paul to mention the name again tomorrow morning, as it was rather important. And indeed he purposed nothing less than writing himself a private and confidential letter from Dombey and Son immediately.

A gong now sounding with great fury, there was a general move towards the dining-room, where every young gentleman had a massive silver fork and a napkin; and all the arrangements were stately and handsome. In particular, there was a butler in a blue coat and bright buttons, who gave quite a winy flavour to the table beer,[2] he poured it out so superbly.

Tea was served in a style no less polite than the dinner; and after tea, the young gentlemen, rising and bowing, withdrew to bed.

There were two sharers of Little Dombey's bedroom—one named Briggs, the other Tozer. In the confidence of that retreat at night, Briggs said his head ached ready to split, and that he should wish himself dead if it wasn't for his mother and a blackbird he had at home. Tozer didn't say very much, but he sighed a good deal, and told Paul to look out, for his turn would come tomorrow. After uttering those prophetic words, he undressed himself moodily, and got into bed.

Paul had sunk into a sweet sleep, and dreamed that he was walking hand in hand with Florence through beautiful gardens, when he

---

1 *dear* Expensive.
2 *table beer* Weak ale.

found that it was a dark, windy morning, with a drizzling rain, and that the gong was giving dreadful note of preparation down in the hall.

So he got up directly, and proceeded softly on his journey downstairs. As he passed the door that stood ajar, a voice from within cried "Is that Dombey?" On Paul replying, "Yes, ma'am"—for he knew the voice to be Miss Blimber's—Miss Blimber said, "Come in, Dombey." And in he went.

"Now, Dombey," said Miss Blimber. "I'm going out for a constitutional."[1]

Paul wondered what that was, and why she didn't send the footman out to get it in such unfavourable weather. But he made no observation on the subject, his attention being devoted to a little pile of new books, on which Miss Blimber appeared to have been recently engaged.

"These are yours, Dombey. I am going out for a constitutional; and while I am gone, that is to say in the interval between this and breakfast, Dombey, I wish you to read over what I have marked in these books, and to tell me if you quite understand what you have got to learn."

They comprised a little English, and a deal of Latin—names of things, declensions of articles and substantives, exercises thereon, and rules—a trifle of orthography, a glance at ancient history, a wink or two at modern ditto,[2] a few tables, two or three weights and measures, and a little general information. When poor Little Dombey had spelt out number two, he found he had no idea of number one; fragments of which afterwards obtruded themselves into number three, which slided into number four, which grafted itself on to number two. So that it was an open question with him whether twenty Romuluses made a Remus,[3] or hic hæc hoc[4] was troy weight, or a verb always agreed with an ancient Briton, or three times four was Taurus a bull.

---

1 *constitutional* Walk taken for the purpose of improving one's health (or physical constitution).

2 *modern ditto* I.e., modern history.

3 *Romuluses made a Remus* In Roman mythology, Romulus and Remus founded the city of Rome.

4 *hic hæc hoc* Latin: this (in its masculine, feminine, and neuter grammatical forms).

"Oh Dombey, Dombey!" said Miss Blimber, when she came back, "this is very shocking, you know."

Miss Blimber expressed herself with a gloomy delight, as if she had expected this result. She divided his books into tasks on subjects A, B, C, and D, and he did very well.

It was hard work, resuming his studies soon after dinner; and he felt giddy and confused and drowsy and dull. But all the other young gentlemen had similar sensations, and were obliged to resume their studies too. The studies went round like a mighty wheel, and the young gentlemen were always stretched upon it.

Such spirits as Little Dombey had he soon lost, of course. But he retained all that was strange and old and thoughtful in his character; and even became more strange and old and thoughtful. He loved to be alone, and liked nothing so well as wandering about the house by himself, or sitting on the stairs listening to the great clock in the hall. He was intimate with all the paper-hanging[1] in the house; he saw things that no one else saw in the patterns; and found out miniature tigers and lions running up the bedroom walls.

The lonely child lived on, surrounded by this arabesque-work of his musing fancy, and no one understood him. Mrs. Blimber thought him "odd," and sometimes the servants said that Little Dombey "moped"; but that was all.

Unless young Toots had some idea on the subject.

He would say to Little Dombey, fifty times a day, "I say—it's of no consequence, you know—but—how are you?"

Little Dombey would answer, "Quite well, sir, thank you."

"Shake hands."

Which Little Dombey, of course, would immediately do. Mr. Toots generally said again, after a long interval of staring and hard breathing, "I say—it's not of the slightest consequence, you know, but I should wish to mention it—how are you, you know?"

To which Little Dombey would again reply, "Quite well, sir, thank you."

One evening a great purpose seemed to flash on Mr. Toots. He went off from his desk to look after[2] Little Dombey, and, finding him

---

1 *paper-hanging* Wallpaper.
2 *look after* Look for.

at the window of his little bedroom, blurted out all at once, as if he were afraid he should forget it: "I say—Dombey—what do you think about?"

"Oh, I think about a great many things."

"*Do* you, though?—I don't, myself."

"I was thinking, when you came in, about last night. It was a beautiful moonlight night. When I had listened to the water for a long time, I got up, and looked out at it. There was a boat over there; the sail like an arm, all silver. It went away into the distance, and what do you think it seemed to do as it moved with the waves?"

"Pitch?"

"It seemed to beckon—seemed to beckon me to come."

This was on a Friday night; it made such a prodigious impression on Mr. Toots, that he had it on his mind as long afterwards as Saturday morning.

And so the solitary child lived on and on, surrounded by the arabesque-work of his musing fancy, and still no one understood him. He grew fond, now, of a large engraving that hung upon the staircase, where, in the centre of a group, one figure that he knew—a figure with a light about its head, benignant, mild, and merciful—stood pointing upward. He watched the waves and clouds at twilight with his earnest eyes, and breasted[1] the window of his solitary room when birds flew by, as if he would have emulated them and soared away.

4

When the midsummer vacation approached, no indecent manifestations of joy were exhibited by the leaden-eyed young gentlemen assembled at Dr. Blimber's. Any such violent expression as "breaking up" would have been quite inapplicable to that polite establishment. The young gentlemen oozed away semi-annually to their own homes, but they never broke up.

Mr. Feeder, B.A., however, seemed to think that he would enjoy the holidays very much. Mr. Toots projected a life of holidays from that time forth; for, as he regularly informed Paul every day, it was his

---

1 *breasted* Faced.

"last half" at Doctor Blimber's, and he was going to begin to come into his property directly.[1]

Mrs. Blimber was by this time quite sure that Paul was the oddest child in the world; and the Doctor did not controvert his wife's opinion. But he said that study would do much; and he said, "Bring him on, Cornelia! Bring him on!"

Cornelia had always brought him on as vigorously as she could; and Paul had had a hard life of it. But, over and above the getting through his tasks, he had long had another purpose always present to him, and to which he still held fast. It was, to be a gentle, useful, quiet little fellow, always striving to secure the love and attachment of the rest; and thus he was an object of general interest—a fragile little plaything that they all liked, and whom no one would have thought of treating roughly.

It was darkly rumoured that even the butler, regarding him with favour such as that stern man had never shown to mortal boy, had mingled porter with his table-beer, to make him strong. But he couldn't change his nature, and so they all agreed that Little Dombey was "old-fashioned."

Over and above other extensive privileges, he had free right of entry to Mr. Feeder's room, from which apartment he had twice led Mr. Toots into the open air in a state of faintness, consequent on an unsuccessful attempt to smoke a very blunt cigar, one of a bundle which that young gentleman had covertly purchased on the shingle[2] from a most desperate smuggler, who had acknowledged, in confidence, that two hundred pounds was the price set upon his head, dead or alive, by the Custom House.

But Mr. Feeder's great possession was a large green jar of snuff, which Mr. Toots had brought down as a present, at the close of the last vacation; and for which he had paid a high price, as having been the genuine property of the Prince Regent. Neither Mr. Toots nor Mr. Feeder could partake of this or any other snuff, even in the most moderate degree, without being seized with convulsions of sneezing. Nevertheless it was their great delight to moisten a box-full with cold tea, stir it up on a piece of parchment with a paper-knife, and devote

---

1   *begin to … property directly* Inherit property in the near future.
2   *shingle* Pebbled beach.

themselves to its consumption then and there. In the course of which cramming of their noses, they endured surprising torments with the constancy of martyrs; and, drinking table beer at intervals, felt all the glories of dissipation.

Going into this room one evening, when the holidays were very near, Paul found Mr. Feeder filling up the blanks in some printed letters, while others were being folded and sealed by Mr. Toots. Mr. Feeder said, "Aha, Dombey, there you are, are you? That's yours."

"Mine, sir?"

"Your invitation, Little Dombey."

Paul, looking at it, found that Doctor and Mrs. Blimber requested the pleasure of Mr. P. Dombey's company at an early party on Wednesday Evening the Seventeenth Instant;[1] and that the hour was half past seven o'clock; and that the object was Quadrilles.[2] He also found that the pleasure of every young gentleman's company was requested by Doctor and Mrs. Blimber on the same genteel occasion.

Mr. Feeder then told him, to his great joy, that his sister was invited, and that he would be expected to inform Doctor and Mrs. Blimber, in superfine small-hand, that Mr. P. Dombey would be happy to have the honour of waiting on them, in accordance with their polite invitation.

Little Dombey thanked Mr. Feeder for these hints, and, pocketing his invitation, sat down on a stool by the side of Mr. Toots, as usual. But Little Dombey's head, which had long been ailing, and was sometimes very heavy, felt so uneasy that night, that he was obliged to support it on his hand. And yet it drooped so, that by little and little it sunk on Mr. Toots's knee, and rested there, as if it had no care to be ever lifted up again.

That was no reason why he should be deaf; but he must have been, he thought, for by and by he heard Mr. Feeder calling in his ear, and gently shaking him to rouse his attention. And when he raised his head, quite scared, and looked about him, he found that Doctor Blimber had come into the room; and that the window was open, and that his forehead was wet with sprinkled water; though how all this had been done without his knowledge, was very curious indeed.

---

1 *Instant* I.e., of this month.
2 *Quadrilles* Card game.

It was very kind of Mr. Toots to carry him to the top of the house so tenderly; and Paul told him that it was. But Mr. Toots said he would do a great deal more than that, if he could; and indeed he did more as it was; for he helped Paul to undress, and helped him to bed, in the kindest manner possible, and then sat down by the bedside and chuckled very much.

How he melted away, and Mr. Feeder changed into Mrs. Pipchin, Paul never thought of asking; but when he saw Mrs. Pipchin standing at the bottom of the bed, instead of Mr. Feeder, he cried out, "Mrs. Pipchin, don't tell Florence!"

"Don't tell Florence what, my little Dombey?"

"About my not being well."

"No, no."

"What do you think I mean to do when I grow up, Mrs. Pipchin?"

Mrs. Pipchin couldn't guess.

"I mean to put my money all together in one bank—never try to get any more—go away into the country with my darling Florence—have a beautiful garden, fields, and woods, and live there with her all my life!"

"Indeed, sir?"

"Yes. That's what I mean to do, when I—" He stopped, and pondered for a moment.

Mrs. Pipchin's grey eye scanned his thoughtful face.

—"If I grow up," said Paul.

There was a certain calm Apothecary, who attended at the establishment, and somehow *he* got into the room and appeared at the bedside. Little Dombey was very chatty with him, and they parted excellent friends. Lying down again with his eyes shut, he heard the Apothecary say that there was a want of vital power (What was that? Paul wondered), and great constitutional weakness. That there was no immediate cause for—what? Paul lost that word. And that the little fellow had a fine mind, but was an old-fashioned boy.

What old fashion could that be, Paul wondered, that was so visibly expressed in him?

He lay in bed all that day, but got up on the next, and went downstairs. Lo and behold, there was something the matter with the great clock; and a workman on a pair of steps had taken its face off, and was poking instruments into the works by the light of a candle! This was a great event for Paul, who sat down on the bottom stair, and watched the operation.

As the workman said, when he observed Paul, "How do you do, sir?" Paul got into conversation with him.

Finding that his new acquaintance was not very well informed on the subject of the Curfew Bell of ancient days,[1] Paul gave him an account of that institution; and also asked him, as a practical man, what he thought about King Alfred's idea of measuring time by the burning of candles.[2] To which the workman replied, that he thought it would be the ruin of the clock trade if it was to come up again. At last the workman put away his tools and went away; though not before he had whispered something, on the door-mat, to the footman, in which there was the phrase "old-fashioned," for Paul heard it.

What could that old fashion be, that seemed to make the people sorry! What could it be!

And now it was that he began to think it must surely be old-fashioned to be very thin and light, and easily tired, and soon disposed to lie down anywhere and rest; for he couldn't help feeling that these were more and more his habits every day.

At last the party-day arrived; and Doctor Blimber said at breakfast, "Gentlemen, we will resume our studies on the twenty-fifth of next month." Mr. Toots immediately threw off his allegiance, and put on a ring: and mentioning the Doctor in casual conversation shortly afterwards, spoke of him as "Blimber"! This act of freedom inspired the older pupils with admiration; but the younger spirits seemed to marvel that no beam fell down and crushed him.

Not the least allusion was made to the ceremonies of the evening, either at breakfast or at dinner; but there was a bustle in the house all day, and Paul made acquaintance with various strange benches and candlesticks, and met a harp in a green great-coat standing on the landing outside the drawing-room door. There was something queer, too, about Mrs. Blimber's head at dinner-time, as if she had screwed her hair up too tight; and though Miss Blimber showed a graceful bunch of plaited hair on each temple, she seemed to have her own

1 *Curfew Bell of ancient days* Used as a means of fire control in medieval England, the Curfew Bell was rung at 8:00 pm nightly as a signal to put out fires and retire to bed.
2 *King Alfred's idea … candles* King Alfred was commonly associated with the invention of the candle clock, a device used to measure the passing of time with a burning candle.

little curls in paper underneath, and in a play-bill too; for Paul read "Theatre Royal" over one of her sparkling spectacles, and "Brighton" over the other.

There was a grand array of white waistcoats and cravats in the young gentlemen's bedrooms as evening approached, and such a smell of singed hair, that Doctor Blimber sent up the footman with his compliments, and wished to know if the house was on fire. But it was only the hairdresser curling the young gentlemen, and over-heating his tongs in the ardour of business.

When Paul was dressed he went down into the drawing-room; where he found Doctor Blimber pacing up and down, full dressed, but with a dignified and unconcerned demeanour, as if he thought it barely possible that one or two people might drop in by and by. Shortly afterwards, Mrs. Blimber appeared, looking lovely, Paul thought, and attired in such a number of skirts that it was quite an excursion to walk round her. Miss Blimber came down soon after her mamma; a little squeezed in appearance, but very charming.

Mr. Toots and Mr. Feeder were the next arrivals. Each of these gentlemen brought his hat in his hand, as if he lived somewhere else; and when they were announced by the butler, Doctor Blimber said, "Ay, ay, ay! God bless my soul!" and seemed extremely surprised to see them. Mr. Toots was one blaze of jewellery and buttons; and he felt the circumstance so strongly, that when he had shaken hands with the Doctor, and had bowed to Mrs. Blimber and Miss Blimber, he took Paul aside, and said, "What do you think of this, Dombey?"

But notwithstanding his modest confidence in himself, Mr. Toots appeared to be involved in a good deal of uncertainty whether, on the whole, it was judicious to button the bottom button of his waistcoat; and whether, on a calm revision of all the circumstances, it was best to wear his wristbands turned up or turned down. Observing that Mr. Feeder's were turned up, Mr. Toots turned his up; but the wristbands of the next arrival being turned down, Mr. Toots turned his down. The differences in point of waistcoat-buttoning, not only at the bottom, but at the top too, became so numerous and complicated as the arrivals thickened, that Mr. Toots was continually fingering that article of dress, as if he were performing on some instrument.

All the young gentlemen, tightly cravatted, curled, and pumped,[1] and with their best hats in their hands, having been at different times announced and introduced, Mr. Baps, the dancing-master, came, accompanied by Mrs. Baps, to whom Mrs. Blimber was extremely kind and condescending.[2] Mr. Baps was a very grave gentleman, and before he had stood under the lamp five minutes he began to talk to Toots (who had been silently comparing pumps with him) about what you were to do with your raw materials when they came into your ports in return for your drain of gold. Mr. Toots, to whom the question seemed perplexing, suggested, "Cook 'em." But Mr. Baps did not appear to think that would do.

Paul now slipped away from the cushioned corner of a sofa, which had been his post of observation, and went down stairs into the tea-room to be ready for Florence. Presently she came, looking so beautiful in her simple ball-dress, with her fresh flowers in her hand, that when she knelt down on the ground to take Paul round the neck and kiss him, he could hardly make up his mind to let her go again.

"But what is the matter, Floy?" asked Paul, almost sure that he saw a tear on her face.

"Nothing, darling; nothing."

Paul touched her cheek gently with his finger—and it *was* a tear! "Why, Floy!"

"We'll go home together, and I'll nurse you, love."

"Nurse me! Floy. Do *you* think I have grown old-fashioned? Because I know they say so, and I want to know what they mean, Floy."

From his nest among the sofa-pillows, where she came at the end of every dance, he could see and hear almost everything that passed at the ball. There was one thing in particular that he observed. Mr. Feeder, after imbibing several custard-cups of negus,[3] began to enjoy himself, and told Mr. Toots that he was going to throw a little spirit into the thing. After that he not only began to dance as if he meant dancing and nothing else, but secretly to stimulate the music[4] to perform wild tunes. Further, he became particular in his attentions to the ladies; and dancing with Miss Blimber, whispered to her—whis-

---

1   *pumped* Wearing pumps, formal shoes of patent leather.
2   *condescending* Considerate, even to those of lower social standing.
3   *negus* Spiced wine.
4   *music* Company of musicians.

pered to her!—though not so softly but that Paul heard him say this remarkable poetry,

> "Had I a heart for falsehood framed,
> I ne'er could injure YOU!"[1]

This, Paul heard him repeat to four young ladies, in succession. Well might Mr. Feeder say to Mr. Toots, that he was afraid he should be the worse for it tomorrow!

A buzz at last went round of "Dombey's going!" "Little Dombey's going!" and there was a general move after him and Florence down the staircase and into the hall.

Once, for a last look, he turned, surprised to see how shining and how bright and numerous the faces were, and how they seemed like a great dream full of eyes.

There was much, soon afterwards—next day, and after that— which Paul could only recollect confusedly. As,[2] why they stayed at Mrs. Pipchin's days and nights, instead of going home.

But he could remember, when he got to his old London home and was carried up the stairs, that there had been the rumbling of a coach for many hours together, while he lay upon the seat, with Florence still beside him, and old Mrs. Pipchin sitting opposite. He remembered his old bed too, when they laid him down in it. But there was something else, and recent, that still perplexed him.

"I want to speak to Florence, if you please. To Florence by herself, for a moment!"

She bent down over him, and the others stood away.

"Floy, my pet, wasn't that papa in the hall, when they brought me from the coach?"

"Yes, dear."

"He didn't cry, and go into his room, Floy, did he, when he saw me coming in?"

She shook her head, and pressed her lips against his cheek.

"I'm very glad he didn't cry, Floy. I thought he did. Don't tell them that I asked."

---

1 *Had I ... injure YOU* Opening lines of an air from Richard Brinsley Sheridan and Thomas Linley's comic opera *The Duenna* (1775).
2 *As* Such as.

The Last.

Little Dombey had never risen from his little bed. He lay there, listening to the noises in the street, quite tranquilly; not caring much how the time went, but watching it and watching everything.

When the sunbeams struck into his room through the rustling blinds, and quivered on the opposite wall, like golden water, he knew that evening was coming on, and that the sky was red and beautiful. As the reflection died away, and a gloom went creeping up the wall, he watched it deepen, deepen, deepen into night. Then he thought how the long unseen streets were dotted with lamps, and how the peaceful stars were shining overhead. His fancy had a strange tendency to wander to the River, which he knew was flowing through the great city; and now he thought how black it was, and how deep it would look reflecting the hosts of stars; and, more than all, how steadily it rolled away to meet the sea.

As it grew later in the night, and footsteps in the street became so rare that he could hear them coming, count them as they passed, and lose them in the hollow distance, he would lie and watch the many-coloured ring about the candle, and wait patiently for day. His only trouble was the swift and rapid river. He felt forced, sometimes, to try to stop it—to stem it with his childish hands, or choke its way with sand; and when he saw it coming on, resistless, he cried out! But a word from Florence, who was always at his side, restored him to himself; and, leaning his poor head upon her breast, he told Floy of his dream, and smiled.

When day began to dawn again, he watched for the sun; and when its cheerful light began to sparkle in the room, he pictured to himself—pictured! he saw—the high church towers rising up into the morning sky, the town reviving, waking, starting into life once more, the river glistening as it rolled (but rolling fast as ever), and the country bright with dew. Familiar sounds and cries came by degrees into the street below; the servants in the house were roused and busy; faces looked in at the door, and voices asked his attendants softly how he was. Paul always answered for himself, "I am better. I am a great deal better, thank you! Tell Papa so!"

By little and little, he got tired of the bustle of the day, the noise of carriages and carts, and people passing and re-passing, and would fall asleep, or be troubled with a restless and uneasy sense again. "Why, will it never stop, Floy?" he would sometimes ask her. "It is bearing me away, I think!"

But she could always soothe and reassure him; and it was his daily delight to make her lay her head down on his pillow, and take some rest.

"You are always watching me, Floy. Let me watch *you*, now!"

They would prop him up with cushions in a corner of his bed, and there he would recline, the while she lay beside him, bending forward often-times to kiss her, and whispering to those who were near, that she was tired, and how she had sat up so many nights beside him.

Thus the flush of the day, in its heat and light, would gradually decline; and again the golden water would be dancing on the wall.

The people around him changed unaccountably, and what had been the Doctor would be his father, sitting with his head leaning on his hand. This figure, with its head leaning on its hand returned so often, and remained so long, and sat so still and solemn, never speaking, never being spoken to, and rarely lifting up its face, that Paul began to wonder languidly if it were real.

"Floy! What *is* that?"

"Where, dearest?"

"There! at the bottom of the bed."

"There's nothing there, except papa!"

The figure lifted up its head and rose, and, coming to the bedside, said:

"My own boy! Don't you know me?"

Paul looked it in the face. Before he could reach out both his hands to take it between them and draw it towards him, the figure turned away quickly from the little bed, and went out at the door.

The next time he observed the figure sitting at the bottom of the bed, he called to it.

"Don't be so sorry for me, dear papa. Indeed, I am quite happy!"

His father coming and bending down to him, he held him round the neck, and repeated those words to him several times, and very earnestly; and he never saw his father in his room again at any time, whether it were day or night, but he called out, "Don't be so sorry for me! Indeed I am quite happy!" This was the beginning of his always saying in the morning that he was a great deal better, and that they were to tell his father so.

How many times the golden water danced upon the wall, how many nights the dark river rolled towards the sea in spite of him, Paul never sought to know. If their kindness, or his sense of it, could have increased, they were more kind, and he more grateful, every day; but whether there were many days or few, appeared of little moment now, to the gentle boy.

One night he had been thinking of his mother and her picture in the drawing-room down stairs. The train of thought suggested to him to inquire if he had ever seen his mother. For he could not remember whether they had told him yes or no; the river running very fast, and confusing his mind.

"Floy, did I ever see mamma?"

"No, darling; why?"

"Did I never see any kind face, like a mamma's, looking at me when I was a baby, Floy?"

"Oh yes, dear!"

"Whose, Floy?"

"Your old nurse's. Often."

"And where is my old nurse? Show me that old nurse, Floy, if you please!"

"She is not here, darling. She shall come tomorrow."

"Thank you, Floy!"

Little Dombey closed his eyes with those words, and fell asleep. When he awoke, the sun was high, and the broad day was clear and warm. Then he awoke—woke mind and body—and sat upright in his bed. He saw them now about him. There was no gray mist before them, as there had been sometimes in the night. He knew them every one, and called them by their names.

"And who is this? Is this my old nurse?" asked the child, regarding with a radiant smile, a figure coming in.

Yes, yes. No other stranger would have shed those tears at sight of him, and called him her dear boy, her pretty boy, her own poor blighted child. No other woman would have stooped down by his bed, and taken up his wasted hand, and put it to her lips and breast, as one who had some right to fondle it. No other woman would have so forgotten everybody there but him and Floy, and been so full of tenderness and pity.

"Floy! this is a kind, good face! I am glad to see it again. Don't go away, old nurse. Stay here! Goodbye!"

"Goodbye, my child?" cried Mrs. Pipchin, hurrying to his bed's head. "Not goodbye?"

"Ah, yes! Goodbye!—Where is papa?"

His father's breath was on his cheek before the words had parted from his lips. The feeble hand waved in the air, as if it cried "Goodbye!" again.

"Now lay me down; and, Floy, come close to me, and let me see you."

Sister and brother wound their arms around each other, and the golden light came streaming in, and fell upon them, locked together.

"How fast the river runs, between its green banks and the rushes, Floy! But, it's very near the sea now. I hear the waves! They always said so!"

Presently he told her that the motion of the boat upon the stream was lulling him to rest. Now the boat was out at sea. And now there was a shore before him. Who stood on the bank!—

He put his hands together, as he had been used to do, at his prayers. He did not remove his arms to do it, but they saw him fold them so, behind his sister's neck.

"Mamma is like you, Floy. I know her by the face! But tell them that the picture on the stairs at school is not Divine enough. The light about the head is shining on me as I go!"

The golden ripple on the wall came back again, and nothing else stirred in the room. The old, old fashion! The fashion that came in with our first garments, and will last unchanged until our race has run its course, and the wide firmament is rolled up like a scroll. The old, old fashion—Death!

Oh, thank GOD, all who see it, for that older fashion yet, of Immortality! And look upon us, Angels of young children, with regards not quite estranged, when the swift river bears us to the ocean!

—1858

Mrs. Gamp

Mr. Pecksniff was in a hackney-cabriolet,[1] for Jonas Chuzzlewit had said, "Spare no expense." It should never be charged upon his father's son that he grudged the money for his father's funeral.

Mr. Pecksniff had been to the undertaker, and was now on his way to another officer in the train of mourning—a female functionary, a nurse, and watcher, and performer of nameless offices about the persons of the dead—whom the undertaker had recommended. Her name, as Mr. Pecksniff gathered from a scrap of writing in his hand, was Gamp; her residence, in Kingsgate Street, High Holborn.[2] So Mr. Pecksniff, in a hackney-cab, was rattling over Holborn's stones, in quest of Mrs. Gamp.

This lady lodged at the bird-fancier's, next door but one to the celebrated mutton-pie shop, and directly opposite to the original cat's-meat[3] warehouse. It was a little house, and this was the more convenient; for Mrs. Gamp being, in her highest walk of art, a monthly nurse,[4] and lodging in the first-floor front, was easily assailable at night by pebbles, walking-sticks, and fragments of tobacco-pipe—all much more efficacious than the street-door knocker; which was so ingeniously constructed as to wake the street with ease, without making the smallest impression on the premises to which it was addressed.

It chanced on this particular occasion that Mrs. Gamp had been up all the previous night. It chanced that Mrs. Gamp had not been regularly engaged, but had been called in at a crisis, in consequence of her great repute, to assist another professional lady with her advice; and it thus happened that, all points of interest in the case being over, Mrs. Gamp had come home again to the bird-fancier's, and gone to bed. So, when Mr. Pecksniff drove up in the hackney-cab, Mrs.

---

1   *hackney-cabriolet* Hired horse-drawn coach.
2   *High Holborn* Street in central London.
3   *bird-fancier* Seller of caged birds; *cat's-meat* Cats in London were fed raw horse meat sold by street venders.
4   *monthly nurse* Woman engaged to care for a mother and baby during the period after the mother has given birth; some also assisted with delivery.

Gamp's curtains were drawn close, and Mrs. Gamp was fast asleep behind them.

Mr. Pecksniff, in the innocence of his heart, applied himself to the knocker; but, at the first double-knock, every window in the street became alive with female heads; and before he could repeat it, whole troops of married ladies came flocking round the steps, all crying out with one accord, and with uncommon interest, "Knock at the winder, sir, knock at the winder. Lord bless you, don't lose no more time than you can help—knock at the winder!"

Borrowing the driver's whip for the purpose, Mr. Pecksniff soon made a commotion among the first-floor flower-pots, and roused Mrs. Gamp, whose voice—to the great satisfaction of the matrons—was heard to say, "I'm coming."

"He's as pale as a muffin," said one lady, in allusion to Mr. Pecksniff.

"So he ought to be, if he's the feelings of a man," observed another.

A third lady said she wished he had chosen any other time for fetching Mrs. Gamp, but it always happened so with *her*.

It gave Mr. Pecksniff much uneasiness to infer, from these remarks, that he was supposed to have come to Mrs. Gamp upon an errand touching, not the close of life, but the other end. Mrs. Gamp herself was under the same impression, for, throwing open the window, she cried behind the curtains, as she hastily dressed herself:

"Is it Mrs. Perkins?"

"No!" returned Mr. Pecksniff, sharply, "nothing of the sort."

"What, Mr. Whilks! Don't say it's you, Mr. Whilks, and that poor creetur Mrs. Whilks with not even a pincushion ready. Don't say it's you, Mr. Whilks!"

"It isn't Mr. Whilks. I don't know the man. Nothing of the kind. A gentleman is dead; and some person being wanted in the house, you have been recommended by Mr. Mould the undertaker. You are also wanted to relieve Mrs. Prig, the day-nurse in attendance on the book-keeper of the deceased—one Mr. Chuffey—whose grief seems to have affected his mind."

As she was by this time in a condition to appear, Mrs. Gamp, who had a face for all occasions, looked out of the window with her mourning countenance, and said she would be down directly.

But the matrons took it very ill that Mr. Pecksniff's mission was of so unimportant a kind; and the lady number three rated him in good round terms, signifying that she would be glad to know what he meant by terrifying delicate females "with his corpses," and giving it as her opinion that he was ugly enough to know better.

The other ladies were not behindhand in expressing similar sentiments; and the children, of whom some scores had now collected, hooted Mr. Pecksniff. So, when Mrs. Gamp appeared, the unoffending gentleman was glad to hustle her with very little ceremony into the cabriolet, and drive off, overwhelmed with popular execration.

Mrs. Gamp had a large bundle with her, a pair of pattens,[1] and a species of gig umbrella; the latter article in colour like a faded leaf, except where a circular patch of a lively blue had been let in at the top. She was much flurried by the haste she had made, and laboured under the most erroneous views of cabriolets, which she appeared to confound with mail-coaches or station-wagons, insomuch that she was constantly endeavouring for the first half-mile to force her luggage through the little front window, and clamouring to the driver to "put it in the boot." When she was disabused of this idea, her whole being resolved itself into an absorbing anxiety about her pattens, with which she played innumerable games at quoits on Mr. Pecksniff's legs. It was not until they were close upon the house of mourning that she had enough composure to observe:

"And so the gentleman's dead, sir! Ah! The more's the pity"—she didn't even know his name. "But it's what we must all come to. It's as certain as being born, except that we can't make our calculations as exact. Ah! Poor dear!"

She was a fat old woman, this Mrs. Gamp, with a husky voice and a moist eye. Having very little neck, it cost her some trouble to look over herself, if one may say so, at those to whom she talked. She wore a rusty black gown, rather the worse for snuff,[2] and a shawl and bonnet to correspond. The face of Mrs. Gamp—the nose in particular—was somewhat red and swollen, and it was difficult to enjoy her society without becoming conscious of a smell of spirits.

"Ah!" repeated Mrs. Gamp, for that was always a safe sentiment in cases of mourning—"ah, dear! When Gamp was summonsed to his

---

1   *pattens* Protective wooden overshoes used to elevate the wearer above unpaved or filthy streets.

2   *rather the worse for snuff* Like other tobacco products, snuff can leave noticeable stains on clothing.

long home, and I see him a lying in the hospital with a penny-piece[1] on each eye, and his wooden leg under his left arm, I thought I should have fainted away. But I bore up."

If certain whispers current in the Kingsgate Street circles had any truth in them, Mrs. Gamp had indeed borne up surprisingly, and had exerted such uncommon fortitude as to dispose of Mr. Gamp's remains for the benefit of science.

"You have become indifferent since then, I suppose? Use is second nature, Mrs. Gamp."

"You may well say second natur, sir. One's first ways is to find sich things a trial to the feelings, and such is one's lasting custom. If it wasn't for the nerve a little sip of liquor gives me (which I was never able to do more than taste it), I never could go through with what I sometimes has to do. 'Mrs. Harris,' I says, at the wery last case as ever I acted in, which it was but a young person—'Mrs. Harris,' I says, 'leave the bottle on the chimley-piece, and don't ask me to take none, but let me put my lips to it when I am so dis-poged, and then I will do what I am engaged to do, according to the best of my ability.' 'Mrs. Gamp,' she says, in answer, 'if ever there was a sober creetur to be got at eighteen-pence a day for working people, and three and six[2] for gentlefolks—night watching being a extra charge—you are that inwallable person.' 'Mrs. Harris,' I says to her, 'don't name the charge, for if I could afford to lay all my fellow-creeturs out for nothink, I would gladly do it, sich is the love I bears 'em.'"

At this point, she was fain to stop for breath. And advantage may be taken of the circumstance, to state that a fearful mystery sur-rounded this lady of the name of Harris, whom no one in the circle of Mrs. Gamp's acquaintance had ever seen; neither did any human being know her place of residence. There were conflicting rumours on the subject; but the prevalent opinion was that she was a phantom of Mrs. Gamp's brain, created for the purpose of holding complimen-tary dialogues with her on all manner of subjects.

"The bottle shall be duly placed on the chimney-piece, Mrs. Gamp, and you shall put your lips to it at your own convenience."

---

1   *penny-piece* Penny coin.
2   *three and six* Three shillings and six pence; a shilling was worth twelve pence.

"Thank you, sir. Which it is a thing as hardly ever occurs with me, unless when I am indispoged, and find my half a pint o' porter settling heavy on the chest. Mrs. Harris often and often says to me, 'Sairey Gamp,' she says, 'you raly do amaze me!' 'Mrs. Harris,' I says to her, 'why so? Give it a name, I beg!' 'Telling the truth then, ma'am,' says Mrs. Harris, 'and shaming him as shall be nameless betwixt you and me, never did I think, till I know'd you, as any woman could sick-nurse and monthly likeways, on the little that you takes to drink.' 'Mrs. Harris,' I says to her, 'none on us knows what we can do till we tries; and wunst *I* thought so, too. But now,' I says, 'my half a pint of porter fully satisfies; perwisin',[1] Mrs. Harris, that it is brought reg'lar, and draw'd mild.'"

The conclusion of this affecting narrative brought them to the house. In the passage they encountered Mr. Mould, the undertaker, a little elderly gentleman, bald, and in a suit of black; with a note-book in his hand, and a face in which a queer attempt at melancholy was at odds with a smirk of satisfaction.

"Well, Mrs. Gamp, and how are *you*, Mrs. Gamp?"

"Pretty well, I thank you, sir."

"You'll be very particular here, Mrs. Gamp. This is not a common case, Mrs. Gamp. Let everything be very nice and comfortable, Mrs. Gamp, if you please."

"It shall be so, sir; you knows me of old, I hope, and so does Mrs. Mould, your ansome pardner, sir; and so does the two sweet young ladies, your darters; although the blessing of a daughter was deniged me, which, if we had had one, Gamp would certainly have drunk its little shoes right off its feet, as with our precious boy he did, and aterwards send the child a errand, to sell his wooden leg for any liquor it would fetch as matches in the rough; which was truly done be-yond his years, for ev'ry individgle penny that child lost at tossing for kidney-pies, and come home aterwards quite bold, to break the news, and offering to drown himself if sech would be a satisfaction to his parents. But wery different is them two sweet young ladies o' yourn, Mister Mould, as I know'd afore a tooth in their pretty heads was cut, and have many a time seen—ah! the dear creeturs!—a playing at berryin's down in the shop, and a follerin' the order-book to its long

---

1 *perwisin'* Providing.

home in the iron safe. Young ladies with such faces as your darters thinks of something else besides berryin's; don't they, sir? Thinks o' marryin's; don't they, sir?"

"I'm sure I don't know, Mrs. Gamp. Very shrewd woman, Mr. Pecksniff, sir. Woman whose intellect is immensely superior to her station in life; sort of woman one would really almost feel disposed to bury for nothing, and do it neatly, too. Mr. Pecksniff, sir. This is one of the most impressive cases, sir, that I have seen in the whole course of my professional experience."

"Indeed, Mr. Mould!"

"Such affectionate regret I never saw. There is no limitation; there is positively NO limitation in point of expense! I have orders, sir, in short, to turn out something absolutely gorgeous."

"My friend Mr. Jonas is an excellent man."

"Well, I have seen a good deal of what is filial in my time, sir, and of what is unfilial, too! It is the lot of parties in my line, sir. We come into the knowledge of those secrets. But anything so filial as this—anything so honourable to human nature, so calculated to reconcile all of us to the world we live in—never yet came under my observation. It only proves, sir, what was so forcibly observed by the lamented poet—buried at Stratford—that there is good in everything."[1]

"It is very pleasant to hear you say so, Mr. Mould."

"You are very kind, sir. And what a man the late Mr. Chuzzlewit was, sir! Ah! what a man he was. Mr. Pecksniff, sir, good morning!"

Mr. Pecksniff returned the compliment; and Mould was going away with a brisk smile, when he remembered the occasion. Quickly becoming depressed again, he sighed; looked into the crown of his hat, as if for comfort; put it on without finding any; and slowly departed.

Mrs. Gamp and Mr. Pecksniff then ascended the staircase; and Mrs. Gamp, having been shown to the chamber in which all that remained of old Anthony Chuzzlewit lay covered up, with but one loving heart, and that the heart of his old book-keeper, to mourn it, left Mr. Pecksniff free to enter the darkened room below in search of Mr. Jonas.

---

1 *there is good in everything* Cf. Shakespeare's *As You Like It* 2.1.12–17.

He found that example to bereaved sons; and pattern in the eyes of all performers of funerals, so subdued, that he could scarcely be heard to speak, and only seen to walk across the room.

"Pecksniff, you shall have the regulation of it all, mind! You shall be able to tell anybody who talks about it, that everything was correctly and freely done. There isn't any one you'd like to ask to the funeral, is there?"

"No, Mr. Jonas, I think not."

"Because if there is, you know, ask him. We don't want to make a secret of it."

"No; I am not the less obliged to you on that account, Mr. Jonas, for your liberal hospitality; but there really is no one."

"Very well; then you, and I, and old Chuffey, and the doctor, will be just a coachful. We'll have the doctor, Pecksniff, because he knows what was the matter with my father, and that it couldn't be helped."

With that, they went up to the room where the old book-keeper was, attended by Mrs. Betsey Prig. And to them entered Mrs. Gamp soon afterwards, who saluted Mrs. Prig as one of the sisterhood, and "the best of creeturs."

The old book-keeper sat beside the bed, with his hands folded before him, and his head bowed down; until Mrs. Gamp took him by the arm, when he meekly rose, saying:

"My old master died at threescore and ten—ought and carry seven. Some men are so strong that they live to fourscore—four times ought's an ought, four times two's an eight—eighty. Oh! why—why—why—didn't he live to four times ought's an ought, and four times two's an eight—eighty? Why did he die before his poor old crazy servant! Take him from me, and what remains? I loved him. He was good to me. I took him down once, six boys, in the arithmetic class at school. God forgive me! Had I the heart to take him down!"

"Well I'm sure," said Mrs. Gamp, "you're a wearing old soul, and that's the blessed truth. You ought to know that you was born in a wale,[1] and that you live in a wale, and that you must take the consequences of sich a sitivation. As a good friend of mine has frequent made remark to me, Mr. Jonage Chuzzlewit, which her name, sir—I will not deceive you—is Harris—Mrs. Harris through the square and

---

1 *wale* I.e., vale, a river valley. A Christian idiom characterizes earthly life as a "vale of tears."

up the steps a turnin' round by the tobacker shop—and which she said it the last Monday evening as ever dawned upon this Pilgrim's Progress[1] of a mortal wale, 'O Sairey, Sairey, little do we know wot lays afore us!' 'Mrs. Harris, ma'am,' I says, 'not much, it's true, but more than you suppoge. Our calcilations, ma'am,' I says, 'respectin' wot the number of a family will be, comes most times within one, and oftener than you would suppoge, exact.' 'Sairey,' says Mrs. Harris, in a awful way, 'tell me wot is my individge number.' 'No, Mrs. Harris,' I says to her, 'ex-cuge me, if you please. My own family,' I says, 'has fallen out of three-pair backs, and has had damp doorsteps settled on their lungs, and one was turned up smilin' in a bedstead unbeknown. Therefore, ma'am,' I says, 'seek not to protigipate, but take 'em as they come and as they go. Mine,' I says to her—'mine is all gone, my dear young chick. And as to husbands, there's a wooden leg gone likewise home to its account, which, in its constancy of walking into public-'ouses, and never coming out again till fetched by force, was quite as weak as flesh, if not weaker.'"

Mrs. Gamp, left to the live part of her task by Mr. Pecksniff and Jonas, now formally relieved Mrs. Prig for the night. That interesting lady had a gruff voice and a beard, and straightway got her bonnet and shawl on.

"Anythink to tell afore you goes, Betsey, my dear?"

"The pickled salmon in this house is delicious. I can partickler recommend it. The drinks is all good. His physic[2] and them things is on the drawers and mankleshelf. He took his last slime draught[3] at seven. The easy-chair ain't soft enough. You'll want his piller."

Mrs. Gamp thanked Mrs. Prig for these friendly hints, and gave her good night. She then composed the patient for sleep—on his rising in bed and rocking himself to and fro with a moan—by screwing her hand into the nape of his neck, administering a dozen or two of hearty shakes, and saying, "Bother the old wictim, what a worriting wexagious creetur it is!"

She then entered on her official duties, in manner following: firstly, she put on a yellow-white nightcap of prodigious size, in shape resem-

---

1 *Pilgrim's Progress* Title of a 1678 Christian allegory by John Bunyan in which characters journey from the material world to heaven.
2 *physic* Medicine.
3 *slime draught* Medicinal drink.

bling a cabbage: having previously divested herself of a row of bald old curls, which could scarcely be called false, they were so innocent of anything approaching to deception; secondly, and lastly, she summoned the housemaid, to whom she delivered this official charge, in tones expressive of faintness:

"I think, young woman, as I could peck a little bit o' pickled salmon, with a little sprig o' fennel, and a sprinkling o' white pepper. I takes new bread, my dear, with a jest a little pat o' fredge butter and a mossel o' cheese. With respect to ale, if they draws the Brighton old tipper at any 'ouse nigh here,[1] I takes that ale at night, my love; not as I cares for it myself, but on accounts of it being considered wakeful by the doctors; and whatever you do, young woman, don't bring me more than a shilling's worth of gin-and-water, warm, when I rings the bell a second time; for that is always my allowange, and I never takes a drop beyond. In case there should be sich a thing as a cowcumber in the 'ouse, I'm rather partial to 'em, though I am but a poor woman. Rich folks may ride on camels, but it ain't so easy for them to see out of a needle's eye.[2] That is my comfort, and I hopes I knows it."

Mrs. Gamp's supper and drink being brought and done full justice to, she administered the patient's medicine by the simple process of clutching his windpipe to make him gasp, and immediately pouring it down his throat.

"I a'most forgot your piller, I declare!" she said, drawing it away. "There! Now you're as comfortable as you need be, I'm sure! and I'm a going to be comfortable too."

All her arrangements made, she lighted the rushlight,[3] coiled herself up on her couch, and fell asleep.

Ghostly and dark the room became, and full of shadows. The noises in the streets were hushed, the house was quiet, the dead of night was coffined in the silent city. When Mrs. Gamp awoke, she found that the busy day was broad awake too. Mrs. Prig relieved punctually, having passed a good night at another patient's. But Mrs. Prig relieved in an ill temper.

---

1 *if they … nigh here* If they serve (on tap) Brighton ale at any pub near here.
2 *Rich folks … needle's eye* Cf. Mark 10.25: "It is easier for a camel to go through the eye of a needle, than for a rich man to enter into the Kingdom of God."
3 *rushlight* Weak candle made from rushes dipped in melted fat.

The best among us have their failings, and it must be conceded of Mrs. Prig, that if there were a blemish in the goodness of her disposition, it was a habit she had of not bestowing all its sharp and acid properties upon her patients (as a thoroughly amiable woman would have done), but of keeping a considerable remainder for the service of her friends. She looked offensively at Mrs. Gamp, and winked her eye. Mrs. Gamp felt it necessary that Mrs. Prig should know her place, and be made sensible of her exact station in society. So she began a remonstrance with—

"Mrs. Harris, Betsey—"

"Bother Mrs. Harris!"

Mrs. Gamp looked at Betsey with amazement, incredulity, and indignation. Mrs. Prig, winking her eye tighter, folded her arms and uttered these tremendous words—

"I don't believe there's no sich a person!"

With these expressions, she snapped her fingers once, twice, thrice, each time nearer to the face of Mrs. Gamp, and then turned away as one who felt that there was now a gulf between them which nothing could ever bridge across.

—1858

David Copperfield

I had known Mr. Peggotty's house very well in my childhood, and I am sure I could not have been more charmed with it if it had been Aladdin's palace, roc's egg and all.[1] It was an old black barge, or boat, high and dry on Yarmouth Sands,[2] with an iron funnel sticking out of it for a chimney. There was a delightful door cut in the side, and it was roofed in, and there were little windows in it. It was beautifully clean, and as tidy as possible. There were some lockers and boxes, and there was a table, and there was a Dutch clock,[3] and there was a chest of drawers, and there was a tea-tray with a painting on it, and the tray was kept from tumbling down by a Bible, and the tray, if it *had* tumbled down, would have smashed a quantity of cups and saucers and a teapot that were grouped around the book. On the walls were coloured pictures of Abraham in red going to sacrifice Isaac in blue; and of Daniel in yellow being cast into a den of green lions.[4] Over the little mantle-shelf was a picture of the "Sarah Jane" lugger,[5] built at Sunderland, with a real little wooden stern stuck on it—a work of art combining composition with carpentry, which I had regarded in my childhood as one of the most enviable possessions the world could afford. Mr. Peggotty, as honest a seafaring man as ever breathed, dealt in lobsters, crabs, and crawfish; and a heap of those creatures, in a state of wonderful conglomeration with one another, and never leaving off pinching whatever they laid hold of, were usually to be found in a little wooden out-house, where the pots and kettles were kept.

As in my childhood, so in these days, when I was a young man, Mr. Peggotty's household consisted of his orphan nephew, Ham Peggotty,

---

1   *Aladdin ... and all* In his tale in *One Thousand and One Nights* (1710), Aladdin's palace is built by a genie and is finer than any other palace. Aladdin requests that the genie bring him the egg of a roc, a giant mythological bird, but the genie refuses.
2   *Yarmouth Sands* Coastal area in the county of Norfolk.
3   *Dutch clock* Simple clock with a plain face and pendulum. Dutch clocks were inexpensive and favored for use by the poor.
4   *Abraham ... green lions* The pictures depict biblical tales. See Genesis 22 and Daniel 6.
5   *lugger* Small sailboat.

a young shipwright; his adopted niece, Little Emily, once my small sweetheart, now a beautiful young woman; and Mrs. Gummidge.

All three had been maintained at Mr. Peggotty's sole charge for years and years, and Mrs. Gummidge was the widow of his partner in a boat, who had died poor. She was very grateful, but she would have been more agreeable company in a small habitation if she had hit upon any other acknowledgement of the hospitality she received than constantly complaining, as she sat in the most comfortable corner by the fireside, that she was a "lone lorn creetur and everythink went contrairy with her."

Towards this old boat I walked one memorable night, with my former schoolfellow and present dear friend, Steerforth—Steerforth, half a dozen years older than I, brilliant, handsome, easy, winning, whom I admired with my whole heart, for whom I entertained the most romantic feelings of fidelity and friendship. He had come down with me from London, and had entered with the greatest ardour into my scheme of visiting the old simple place, and the old simple people.

There was no moon, and as he and I walked on the dark, wintry sands, towards the old boat, the wind sighed mournfully.

"This is a wild place, Steerforth, is it not?"

"Dismal enough in the dark, and the sea has a cry in it, as if it were hungry for us. Is that the boat, where I see a light yonder?"

"That's the boat."

We said no more as we approached the light, but made softly for the door. I laid my hand upon the latch, and, whispering Steerforth to keep close to me, went in, and I was in the midst of the astonished family, whom I had not seen from my childhood, face to face with Mr. Peggotty, and holding out my hand to him, when Ham shouted, "Mas'r Davy! it's Mas'r Davy!"

In a moment we were all shaking hands with one another, and asking one another how we did, and telling one another how glad we were to meet, and all talking at once. Mr. Peggotty was so overjoyed to see me, and to see my friend, that he did not know what to say or do, but kept over and over again shaking hands with me, and then with Steerforth, and then with me, and then ruffling his shaggy hair all over his head, and then laughing with such glee and triumph, that it was a treat to see him.

"Why, that you two gentl'men—gentl'men growed—should come to this here roof to-night, of all nights in my life, is such a merry-go-rounder as never happened afore, I do rightly believe. Em'ly, my darling, come here. Come here, my little witch. Theer's Mas'r Davy's friend, my dear! Theer's the gentl'man as you've heerd on, Em'ly. He comes to see you along with Mas'r Davy, on the brightest night of your uncle's life as ever was or will be; horroar[1] for it!" Then he let her go, and, as she ran into her little chamber, looked round upon us, quite hot and out of breath with his uncommon satisfaction.

"If you two gentl'men—gentl'men growed now, and such gentl'men—don't ex-cuse me for being in a state of mind, when you understand matters, I'll arks your pardon. Em'ly, my dear! She knows I'm going to tell, and has made off. This here little Em'ly, sir," to Steerforth, "her as you see a blushing here just now—this here little Em'ly of ours has been in our house, sir, what I suppose (I'm a ignorant man, but that's my belief) no one but a little bright-eyed creetur *can* be in a house. She ain't my child, I never had one; but I couldn't love her more if she was fifty times my child. You understand; I couldn't do it!"

"I quite understand."

"I know you do, sir, and thank'ee. Well, sir, there was a certain person as had know'd our Em'ly from the time when her father was drownded; as had seen her constant when a babby, when a young gal, when a woman. Not much of a person to look at, he warn't—something o' my own build, rough, a good deal o' the sou'wester in him, wery salt, but, on the whole, a honest sort of a chap too, with his art in the right place."

I had never seen Ham grin to anything like the extent to which he sat grinning at us now.

"What does this here blessed tarpaulin go and do, but he loses that there art of his to our little Em'ly. He follers her about, he makes his-self a sort o' servant to her, he loses in a great measure his relish for his wittles, and, in the long run, he makes it clear to me wot's amiss.

"Well, I counsels him to speak to Em'ly. He's big enough, but he's bashfuller than a little un, and he says to me he doen't like. So I speak. 'What, *him*!' says Em'ly, '*him* that I've know'd so intimate so many

---

1 *horroar* Hooray.

year, and like so much? Oh, Uncle! I never can have *him*! He's such a good fellow!' I gives her a kiss, and I says no more to her than, 'My dear, you're right to speak out, you're to choose for yourself, you're as free as a little bird.' Then I aways to him, and I says, 'I wish it could have been so, but it can't. But you can both be as you was, and wot I say to you is, Be as you was with her, like a man.' He says to me, a shaking of my hand, 'I will,' he says. And then he was, honourable, trew, and manful, going on for two year.

"All of a sudden, one evening, as it might be to-night, comes little Em'ly from her work, and him with her! There ain't so much in *that*, you'll say. No, sure, because he takes care on her, like a brother, arter dark, and indeed afore dark, and at all times. But this heer tarpaulin chap, he takes hold of her hand, and he cries out to me, joyful, 'Look'ee here! This is to be my little wife!' And she says, half bold and half shy, and half a laughing, and half a crying, 'Yes, uncle! If you please.' If I please! Lord, as if I should do anythink else! 'If you please,' she says, 'I am steadier now, and I have thought better of it, and I'll be as good a little wife as I can to him, for he's a dear good fellow!' Then Missis Gummidge, she claps her hands like a play, and you come in. There, the murder's out![1] You come in! It took place this here present hour, and here's the man as'll marry her the minute she's out of her time at the needlework."

Ham staggered, as well he might, under the blow Mr. Peggotty dealt him, as a mark of confidence and friendship; but, feeling called upon to say something to us, he stammered:

"She warn't no higher than you was, Mas'r Davy, when you first come heer, when I thought what she'd grow up to be. I see her grow up, gentl'men, like a flower. I'd lay down my life for her, Mas'r Davy— Oh, most content and cheerful. There ain't a gentl'man in all the land, nor yet a sailing upon all the sea—that can love his lady more than I love her, though there's many a common man as could say better what he meant."

I thought it affecting to see such a sturdy fellow trembling in the strength of what he felt for the pretty little creature who had won his heart. I thought the simple confidence reposed in us by Mr. Peggotty, and by himself, was touching. I was affected by the story altogether.

---

1 *murder's out* Secret is revealed.

I was filled with pleasure, but at first with an indescribably sensitive pleasure, that a very little would have changed to pain.

Therefore, if it had depended upon me to touch the prevailing chord among them, with any skill, I should have made a poor hand of it. But it depended upon Steerforth, and he did it with such address, that in a few minutes we were all as easy as possible.

"Mr. Peggotty," he said, "you are a thoroughly good fellow, and deserve to be as happy as you are to-night. My hand upon it. Ham, I give you joy, my boy. My hand upon that, too! Davy, stir the fire and make it a brisk one. And, Mr. Peggotty, unless you can induce your gentle niece to come back, I shall go. Any gap at your fireside on such a night—such a gap, least of all—I wouldn't make for the wealth of the Indies."

So Mr. Peggotty went to fetch little Em'ly. At first little Em'ly didn't like to come, and then Ham went. Presently they brought her to the fireside, very much confused, and very shy; but she soon became more assured when she found how Steerforth spoke to her; how skilfully he avoided anything that would embarrass her; how he talked to Mr. Peggotty of boats, and ships, and tides, and fish; how delighted he was with that boat and all belonging to it; how lightly and easily he carried on, until he brought us by degrees into a charmed circle.

But he set up no monopoly of the conversation. He was silent and attentive when little Em'ly talked across the fire to me of our old childish wanderings upon the beach, to pick up shells and pebbles; he was very silent and attentive when I asked her if she recollected how I used to love her, and how we used to walk about that dim old flat, hours and hours, and how the days sported by us as if Time himself had not grown up then, but were a child like ourselves, and always at play. She sat all the evening in her old little corner by the fire—Ham beside her. I could not satisfy myself whether it was in her little tormenting way, or in a maidenly reserve before us, that she kept quite close to the wall, and away from Ham; but I observed that she did so all the evening.

As I remember, it was almost midnight when we took our leave. We had had some biscuit and dried fish for supper, and Steerforth had produced from his pocket a flask of Hollands.[1] We parted mer-

---

1 *Hollands* Type of gin made in Holland.

rily; and as they all stood crowded round the door to light us on our road, I saw the sweet blue eyes of little Em'ly peeping after us, from behind Ham, and heard her soft voice calling to us to be careful how we went.

"A most engaging little beauty!" said Steerforth, taking my arm. "Well! It's a quaint place, and they are quaint company; and it's quite a new sensation to mix with them."

"How fortunate we are, too, Steerforth, to have arrived to witness their happiness in that intended marriage! I never saw people so happy. How delightful to see it!"

"Yes—that's rather a chuckle-headed[1] fellow for the girl. Isn't he?"

I felt a shock in this cold reply. But turning quickly upon him, and seeing a laugh in his eyes, I answered:

"Ah, Steerforth! It's well for you to joke about the poor! But when I see how perfectly you understand them, and how you can enter into happiness like this plain fisherman's, I know there is not a joy, or sorrow, or any emotion of such people that can be indifferent to you. And I admire and love you for it, Steerforth, twenty times the more!"

To my surprise he suddenly said, with nothing that I could see to lead to it:

"Daisy, I wish to God I had had a judicious father these last twenty years! You know my mother has always doted on me and spoilt me. I wish with all my soul I had been better guided! I wish with all my soul I could guide myself better!"

There was a passionate dejection in his manner that quite amazed me. He was more unlike himself than I could have supposed possible.

"It would be better to be this poor Peggotty, or his lout of a nephew, than be myself, twenty times richer and twenty times wiser, and be the torment to myself that I have been in that Devil's bark of a boat within the last half-hour."

I was so confounded by the change in him that at first I could only regard him in silence as he walked at my side. At length I asked him to tell me what had happened to cross him so unusually.

"Tut, it's nothing—nothing, Davy! I must have had a nightmare, I think. What old women call the horrors have been creeping over me from head to foot. I have been afraid of myself."

---

1 *chuckle-headed* Block-headed, stupid.

"You are afraid of nothing else, I think."

"Perhaps not, and yet may have enough to be afraid of too. Well! so it goes by! Daisy—for though that's not the name your godfathers and godmothers gave you, you're such a fresh fellow that it's the name I best like to call you by—and I wish, I wish, I wish you could give it to me!"

"Why, so I can, if I choose."

"Daisy, if anything should ever happen to separate us, you must think of me at my best, old boy. Come! let us make that bargain. Think of me at my best, if circumstances should ever part us."

"You have no best to me, Steerforth, and no worst. You are always equally loved and cherished in my heart."

I was up to go away alone next morning with the dawn, and, having dressed as quietly as I could, looked into his room. He was fast asleep, lying easily with his head upon his arm, as I had often seen him lie at school.

The time came in its season, and that was very soon, when I almost wondered that nothing troubled his repose, as I looked at him then. But he slept—let me think of him so again—as I had often seen him sleep at school; and thus, in this silent hour, I left him.

Nevermore, oh God forgive you, Steerforth! to touch that passive hand in love and friendship. Never, never more!

Chapter 2

Some months elapsed before I again found myself down in that part of the country and approaching the old boat by night.

It was a dark evening, and rain was beginning to fall, when I came within sight of Mr. Peggotty's house, and of the light within it shining through the window. A little floundering across the sand, which was heavy, brought me to the door, and I went in.

I was bidden to a little supper; Em'ly was to be married to Ham that day fortnight,[1] and this was the last time I was to see her in her maiden life.

---

1   *that day fortnight* In exactly two weeks.

It looked very comfortable indeed. Mr. Peggotty had smoked his evening pipe, and there were preparations for supper by and by. The fire was bright, the ashes were thrown up, the locker was ready for little Em'ly in her old place. Mrs. Gummidge appeared to be fretting a little in her own corner, and consequently looked quite natural.

"You're first of the lot, Mas'r Davy! Sit ye down, sir. It ain't o' no use saying welcome to you; but you're welcome, kind and hearty."

Here Mrs. Gummidge groaned.

"Cheer up, cheer up, Mrs. Gummidge!" said Mr. Peggotty.

"No, no, Dan'l. It ain't o' no use telling me to cheer up, when everythink goes contrairy with me. Nothink's nat'ral to me but to be lone and lorn."

After looking at Mrs. Gummidge for some moments with great sympathy, Mr. Peggotty glanced at the Dutch clock, rose, snuffed the candle, and put it in the window.

"Theer! theer we are, Missis Gummidge!" Mrs. Gummidge slightly groaned again. "Theer we are, Mrs. Gummidge, lighted up accordin' to custom! You're a wonderin' what that's fur, sir! Well, it's for our little Em'ly. You see, the path ain't over light or cheerful arter dark; and when I'm here at the hour as she's a comin' home from her needlework down town, I puts the light in the winder. That, you see, meets two objects. She says to herself, says Em'ly, 'Theer's home!' she says. And likeways, says Em'ly, 'My uncle's theer!' Fur if I ain't theer, I never have no light showed. You may say this is like a babby, sir. Well, I doen't know but what I am a babby in regard o' Em'ly. Not to look at, but to—to consider on, you know. I doen't care, bless you! Now I tell you. When I go a looking and looking about that theer pritty house of our Em'ly's, all got ready for her to be married, if I doen't feel as if the littlest things was her, a'most. I takes 'em up, and I puts 'em down, and I touches of 'em as delicate as if they was our Em'ly. So 't is with her little bonnets and that. I couldn't see one on 'em rough used, a purpose, not fur the whole wureld.

"It's my opinion, you see, as this is along of my havin' played with Em'ly so much when she was a child, and havin' made believe as we was Turks, and French, and sharks, and every wariety of forinners—bless you, yes; and lions and whales, and I don't know what all!—when she warn't no higher than my knee. I've got into the way on it, you know. Why, this here candle, now! I know wery well that arter she's married and gone, I shall put that candle theer, just the same as now, and sit afore the fire, pretending I'm expecting of her, like as I'm a doing now. Why, at the present minute when I see the candle sparkle up, I says to myself, 'She's a looking at it! Em'ly's a coming!' Right too, fur here she is!"

No; it was only Ham. The night should have turned more wet since I came in, for he had a large sou'wester hat on, slouched over his face.

"Where's Em'ly?"

Ham made a movement as if she were outside. Mr. Peggotty took the light from the window, trimmed it, put it on the table, and was stirring the fire, when Ham, who had not moved, said, "Mas'r Davy, will you come out a minute, and see what Em'ly and me has got to show you?"

As I passed him, I saw to my astonishment and fright that he was deadly pale. He closed the door upon us. Only upon us two.

"Ham! What's the matter?"

"My love, Mas'r Davy—the pride and hope of my art—her that I'd have died for, and would die for now—she's gone!"

"Gone!"

"Em'ly's run away! You're a scholar and know what's right and best. What am I to say, in-doors? How am I ever to break it to him, Mas'r Davy?"

I saw the door move, and tried to hold the latch, to gain a moment's time. It was too late. Mr. Peggotty thrust forth his face; and never could I forget the change that came upon it when he saw us, if I were to live five hundred years.

I remember a great wail and cry, and the women hanging about him, and we all standing in the room—I with an open letter in my hand which Ham had given me; Mr. Peggotty with his vest torn open, his hair wild, his face and lips white, and blood trickling down his bosom (it had sprung from his mouth, I think).

"Read it, sir; slow, please. I doen't know as I can understand."

In the midst of the silence of death, I read thus, from the blotted letter Ham had given me. In Em'ly's hand, addressed to himself:

"'When you, who love me so much better than I ever have deserved, even when my mind was innocent, see this, I shall be far away. When I leave my dear home—my dear home—Oh, my dear home!—in the morning,'" (the letter bore date on the previous night), "'it will be never to come back, unless he brings me back a lady. This will be found at night, many hours after, instead of me. For mercy's sake, tell uncle that I never loved him half so dear as now. Oh, don't remember you and I were ever to be married, but try to think as if I died when I was very little, and was buried somewhere. Pray Heaven that I am going away from, have compassion on my uncle! Be his comfort. Love some good girl, that will be what I was once to uncle, and that will be true to you, and worthy of you, and know no shame but me. God bless all! If he don't bring me back a lady, and I don't pray for my own self, I'll pray for all. My parting love to uncle. My last tears, and my last thanks, for uncle!'" That was all.

He stood, long after I had ceased to read, still looking at me. Slowly at last he moved his eyes from my face, and cast them round the room.

"Who's the man? I want to know his name." Ham glanced at me, and suddenly I felt a shock. "Mas'r Davy! Go out a bit, and let me tell him what I must. You doen't ought to hear it, sir."

I sank down in a chair and tried to utter some reply; but my tongue was fettered, and my sight was weak. For I felt that the man was my friend, the friend I had unhappily introduced there—Steerforth, my old schoolfellow and my friend.

"I want to know his name!"

"Mas'r Davy, it ain't no fault of yourn—and I am far from laying of it to you—but it is your friend Steerforth, and he's a damned villain!"

Mr. Peggotty moved no more, until he seemed to wake all at once, and pulled down his rough coat from its peg in a corner.

"Bear a hand with this! I'm struck of a heap,[1] and can't do it. Bear a hand and help me. Well! Now give me that theer hat!"

Ham asked him whither he was going.

"I'm a going to seek my niece. I'm a going to seek my Em'ly. I'm a going, first, to stave in that theer boat as he gave me, and sink it where I would have drownded *him*, as I'm a livin' soul, if I had had one thought of what was in him! As he sat afore me, in that boat, face to

---

1 *struck of a heap* Extremely disconcerted.

face, strike me down dead, but I'd have drownded him, and thought it right!—I'm a going fur to seek my niece."

"Where?"

"Anywhere! I'm a going to seek my niece through the wureld. I'm a going to find my poor niece in her shame, and bring her back wi' my comfort and forgiveness. No one stop me! I tell you I'm a going to seek my niece! I'm a going to seek her fur and wide!"

Mrs. Gummidge came between them in a fit of crying. "No, no, Dan'l, not as you are now. Seek her in a little while, my lone lorn Dan'l, and that'll be but right; but not as you are now. Sit ye down, and give me your forgiveness for having ever been a worrit to you, Dan'l—what have *my* contraries ever been to this!—and let us speak a word about them times when she was first a orphan, and when Ham was too, and when I was a poor widder woman and you took me in. It'll soften your poor heart, Dan'l, and you'll bear your sorrow better; for you know the promise, Dan'l, 'As you have done it unto one of the least of these, you have done it unto me';[1] and that can never fail under this roof, that's been our shelter for so many, many year!"

He was quite passive now; and when I heard him crying, the impulse that had been upon me to go down upon my knees and curse Steerforth yielded to a better feeling. My overcharged heart found the same relief as his, and I cried too.

Chapter 3

At this period of my life I lived in my top set of chambers in Buckingham Street, Strand, London, and was over head and ears in love with Dora. I lived principally on Dora and coffee. My appetite languished, and I was glad of it, for I felt as though it would have been an act of perfidy towards Dora to have a natural relish for my dinner. I bought four sumptuous waistcoats—not for myself, I had no pride in them—for Dora. I took to wearing straw-coloured kid gloves in the streets. I laid the foundations of all the corns I have ever had. If the boots I wore at that period could only be produced, and compared

---

1 '*As you ... unto me*' In Matthew 25.40, it is said that Christ will speak these words to the righteous regarding their charitable acts.

with the natural size of my feet, they would show in a most affecting manner what the state of my heart was.

Mrs. Crupp, the housekeeper of my chambers, must have been a woman of penetration; for when this attachment was but a few weeks old she found it out. She came up to me one evening when I was very low, to ask (she being afflicted with spasms) if I could oblige her with a little tincture of cardamums, mixed with rhubarb, and flavoured with seven drops of the essence of cloves; or, if I had not such a thing by me, with a little brandy. As I had never even heard of the first remedy, and always had the second in the closet, I gave Mrs. Crupp a glass of the second, which (that I might have no suspicion of its being devoted to any improper use) she began to take immediately.

"Cheer up, sir," said Mrs. Crupp. "Excuse me; I know what it is, sir. There's a lady in the case."

"Mrs. Crupp?"

"Oh, bless you! Keep a good heart, sir! Never say die, sir! If she don't smile upon you, there's a many as will. You're a young gentleman to *be* smiled on, Mr. Copperfull, and you must learn your walue, sir."

Mrs. Crupp always called me Mr. Copperfull: firstly, no doubt, because it was not my name; and secondly, I am inclined to think, in some indistinct association with a washing-day.[1]

"What makes you suppose there is any young lady in the case, Mrs. Crupp?"

"Mr. Copperfull, I'm a mother myself. Your boots and your waist is equally too small, and you don't eat enough, sir, nor yet drink. Sir, I have laundressed other young gentlemen besides you. It was but the gentleman which died here before yourself that fell in love—with a barmaid—and had his waistcoats took in directly, though much swelled by drinking."

"Mrs. Crupp, I must beg you not to connect the young lady in my case with a barmaid, or anything of that sort, if you please."

"Mr. Copperfull, I'm a mother myself, and not likely. I ask your pardon, sir, if I intrude. I should never wish to intrude where I were not welcome. But you are a young gentleman, Mr. Copperfull, and

---

1 *association with a washing-day* Large copper vessels called "coppers" were used to do laundry.

my adwice to you is, to cheer up, sir, to keep a good heart, and to know your own walue. If you was to take to something, sir—if you was to take to skittles,[1] now, which is healthy—you might find it divert your mind, and do you good."

I turned it off, and changed the subject by informing Mrs. Crupp that I wished to entertain at dinner next day my esteemed friend Traddles and Mr. and Mrs. Micawber; and I took the liberty of suggesting a pair of soles,[2] a small leg of mutton, and a pigeon-pie. Mrs. Crupp broke out into rebellion on my first bashful hint in reference to *her* cooking the fish and joint. But, in the end, a compromise was effected, and Mrs. Crupp consented to achieve this feat on condition that I dined from home for a fortnight afterwards.

Having laid in the materials for a bowl of punch, to be compounded by Mr. Micawber, having provided a bottle of lavender-water,[3] two wax candles, a paper of mixed pins, and a pincushion, to assist Mrs. Micawber in her toilette, at my dressing-table, having also caused the fire in my bed-room to be lighted for Mrs. Micawber's convenience, and having laid the cloth with my own hands, I awaited the result with composure.

At the appointed time my three visitors arrived together. Mr. Micawber, with more shirt-collar[4] than usual, and a new ribbon to his eye-glass; Mrs. Micawber, with her cap in a parcel; Traddles carrying the parcel, and supporting Mrs. Micawber on his arm. They were all delighted with my residence. When I conducted Mrs. Micawber to my dressing-table, and she saw the scale on which it was prepared for her, she was in such raptures that she called Mr. Micawber to come in and look.

"My dear Copperfield," said Mr. Micawber, "this is luxurious. This is a way of life which reminds me of the period when I was myself in a state of celibacy. I am at present established on what may be designated as a small and unassuming scale; but you are aware that I have, in the course of my career, surmounted difficulties and conquered obstacles. You are no stranger to the fact that there have been periods of my life, when it has been requisite that I should pause until certain

---

1   *skittles* Game in which the object is to knock over a set of pins.
2   *a pair of soles* Two filets of sole.
3   *lavender-water* Perfume.
4   *more shirt-collar* I.e., a higher collar.

expected events should turn up—when it has been necessary that I should fall back before making what I trust I shall not be accused of presumption in terming—a spring. The present is one of those momentous stages in the life of man. You find me fallen back *for* a spring, and I have every reason to believe that a vigorous leap will shortly be the result."

I informed Mr. Micawber that I relied upon him for a bowl of punch, and led him to the lemons. I never saw a man so thoroughly enjoy himself, as he stirred, and mixed, and tasted, and looked as if he were making, not mere punch, but a fortune for his family down to the latest posterity. As to Mrs. Micawber, I don't know whether it was the effect of the cap, or the lavender-water, or the pins, or the fire, or the wax candles, but she came out of my room, comparatively speaking, lovely.

I suppose—I never ventured to inquire, but I suppose—that Mrs. Crupp, after frying the soles, was taken ill. Because we broke down at that point. The leg of mutton came up very red inside, and very pale outside, besides having a foreign substance of a gritty nature sprinkled over it, as if it had had a fall into ashes. But we were not in a condition to judge of this fact from the appearance of the gravy, forasmuch as it had been all dropped on the stairs. The pigeon-pie was not bad, but it was a delusive pie, the crust being like a disappointing phrenological[1] head—full of lumps and bumps, with nothing particular underneath. In short, the banquet was such a failure that I should have been quite unhappy—about the failure I mean, for I was always unhappy about Dora—if I had not been relieved by the great good-humour of my company.

"My dear friend Copperfield," said Mr. Micawber, "accidents will occur in the best-regulated families, and especially in families not regulated by that pervading influence which sanctifies while it enhances the—a—I would say, in short, by the influence of Woman in the lofty character of Wife. If you will allow me to take liberty of remarking that there are few comestibles better, in their way, than a Devil,[2] and that I believe, with a little division of labour, we could accomplish a good one if the young person in attendance could produce

---

1   *phrenological* Phrenology is the study of bumps and dents on the surface of the skull as a supposed indicator of personality and abilities.
2   *Devil* Meat dish served with devil sauce.

a gridiron,[1] I would put it to you, that this little misfortune may be easily repaired."

There *was* a gridiron in the pantry, on which my morning rasher of bacon was cooked. We had it out in a twinkling. Traddles cut the mutton into slices; Mr. Micawber covered them with pepper, mustard, salt, and cayenne; I put them on the gridiron, turned them with a fork, and took them off, under Mr. Micawber's direction; and Mrs. Micawber heated some mushroom ketchup in a little saucepan. Under these circumstances my appetite came back miraculously. I am ashamed to confess it, but I really believe I forgot Dora for a little while.

"Punch, my dear Copperfield," said Mr. Micawber, tasting it as soon as dinner was done, "like time and tide, waits for no man. Ah! it is at the present moment in high flavour. My love, will you give me your opinion?"

Mrs. Micawber pronounced it excellent.

"As we are quite confidential here, Mr. Copperfield," said Mrs. Micawber, sipping her punch, "(Mr. Traddles being a part of our domesticity), I should much like to have your opinion on Mr. Micawber's prospects. I have consulted branches of my family on the course most expedient for Mr. Micawber to take, and it was, that he should immediately turn his attention to coals."

"To what, ma'am?"

"To coals. To the coal trade. Mr. Micawber was induced to think, on inquiry, that there might be an opening for a man of his talent in the Medway Coal Trade. Then, as Mr. Micawber very properly said, the first step to be taken clearly was to go and *see* the Medway; which we went and saw. I say 'we,' Mr. Copperfield; for I never will desert Mr. Micawber. I am a wife and mother, and I never will desert Mr. Micawber." Traddles and I murmured our admiration. "That," said Mrs. Micawber, "that, at least, is *my* view, my dear Mr. Copperfield and Mr. Traddles, of the obligation which I took upon myself when I repeated the irrevocable words, 'I, Emma, take thee, Wilkins.' I read the service over with a flat candle, on the previous night, and the conclusion I derived from it was that I never could or would desert Mr. Micawber."

---

1   *gridiron* Metal grate used for grilling over a fire.

"My dear," said Mr. Micawber, a little impatiently, "I am not conscious that you are expected to do anything of the sort."

"We went," repeated Mrs. Micawber, "and saw the Medway. My opinion of the coal trade on that river was, that it might require talent, but that it certainly requires capital. Talent, Mr. Micawber has; capital, Mr. Micawber has not. We saw, I think, the greater part of the Medway; and that was my individual conclusion. My family were then of opinion that Mr. Micawber should turn his attention to corn—on commission. But corn, as I have repeatedly said to Mr. Micawber, may be gentlemanly, but it is not remunerative. Commission to the extent of two and ninepence[1] in a fortnight cannot, however limited our ideas, be considered remunerative."

We were all agreed upon that.

"Then," said Mrs. Micawber, who prided herself on taking a clear view of things, and keeping Mr. Micawber straight by her woman's wisdom, when he might otherwise go a little crooked, "then I naturally look round the world, and say, 'What is there in which a person of Mr. Micawber's talent is likely to succeed?' I may have a conviction that Mr. Micawber's manners peculiarly qualify him for the Banking business. I may argue within myself, that if I had a deposit in a banking-house, the manners of Mr. Micawber, as representing that banking-house, would inspire confidence and extend the connexion. But if the various banking-houses refuse to avail themselves of Mr. Micawber's abilities, or receive the offer of them with contumely,[2] what is the use of dwelling upon *that* idea? None. As to originating a banking business, I may know that there are members of my family, who, if they chose to place their money in Mr. Micawber's hands, might found an establishment of that description. But if they do *not* choose to place their money in Mr. Micawber's hands—which they don't—what is the use of that? Again I contend that we are no farther advanced than we were before."

I shook my head, and said, "Not a bit." Traddles also shook his head, and said, "Not a bit."

"What do I deduce from this?" Mrs. Micawber went on to say, still with the same air of putting a case lucidly. "What is the conclusion,

---

1   *two and ninepence* Two shillings and nine pence; a shilling was worth twelve pence.
2   *contumely* Insulting language or treatment.

my dear Mr. Copperfield, to which I am irresistibly brought. Am I wrong in saying it is clear that we must live?"

I answered, "Not at all!" and Traddles answered, "Not at all!" and I found myself afterwards sagely adding, alone, that a person must either live or die.

"Just so," returned Mrs. Micawber. "It is precisely that. And here is Mr. Micawber without any suitable position or employment. Where does that responsibility rest? Clearly on society. Then I would make a fact so disgraceful known, and boldly challenge society to set it right. It appears to me, my dear Mr. Copperfield, that what Mr. Micawber has to do is to throw down the gauntlet to society and say, in effect, 'Show me who will take that up. Let the party immediately step forward.'"

I ventured to ask Mrs. Micawber how this was to be done.

"By advertising in all the papers. It appears to me, that what Mr. Micawber has to do, in justice to himself, in justice to his family, and I will even go so far as to say in justice to society, by which he has been hitherto overlooked, is to advertise in all the papers; to describe himself plainly as so and so, with such and such qualifications, and to put it thus: '*Now* employ me on remunerative terms, and address, post paid, to W.M., Post Office, Camden Town.'[1]

"Advertising is rather expensive," I remarked.

"Exactly so!" said Mrs. Micawber, preserving the same logical air. "Quite true, my dear Mr. Copperfield. I have made the identical observation to Mr. Micawber. It is for that reason, especially, that I think Mr. Micawber ought to raise a certain sum of money—on a bill."[2]

Mr. Micawber, leaning back in his chair, trifled with his eye-glass, and cast his eye up at the ceiling; but I thought him observant of Traddles, too, who was looking at the fire.

"If no member of my family," said Mrs. Micawber, "is possessed of sufficient natural feeling to negotiate that bill—I believe there is a better business term to express what I mean—"

---

1 *Camden Town* District of inner London, considered an unfashionable location in the nineteenth century.

2 *bill* I.e., accommodation bill, a signed document similar in form to a check but serving to raise money on credit, by which the borrower contracts to pay a specific sum at a given date, typically some months in the future.

Mr. Micawber, with his eyes still cast up at the ceiling, suggested, "Discount."[1]

"To discount that bill, then, my opinion is, that Mr. Micawber should go into the city, should take that bill into the money market,[2] and should dispose of it for what he can get."

I felt, but I am sure I don't know why, that this was highly self-denying and devoted in Mrs. Micawber, and I uttered a murmur to that effect. Traddles, who took his tone from me, did likewise, and really I felt that she was a noble woman—the sort of woman who might have been a Roman matron, and done all manner of troublesome heroic public actions.

In the fervour of this impression, I congratulated Mr. Micawber on the treasure he possessed. So did Traddles. Mr. Micawber extended his hand to each of us in succession, and then covered his face with his pocket-handkerchief—which I think had more snuff upon it than he was aware of. He then returned to the punch in the highest state of exhilaration.

Mrs. Micawber made tea for us in a most agreeable manner, and after tea we discussed a variety of topics before the fire; and she was good enough to sing us (in a small, thin, flat voice, which I remembered to have considered, when I first knew her, the very table-beer[3] of acoustics) the favourite ballads of "The Dashing White Sergeant" and "Little Tafflin." For both of these songs Mrs. Micawber had been famous when she lived at home with her papa and mamma. Mr. Micawber told us that when he heard her sing the first one, on the first occasion of his seeing her beneath the parental roof, she had attracted his attention in an extraordinary degree; but that when it came to "Little Tafflin" he had resolved to win that woman or perish in the attempt.

It was between ten and eleven o'clock when Mrs. Micawber rose to replace her cap in the parcel, and to put on her bonnet. Mr. Micawber took the opportunity to slip a letter into my hand, with a whispered

---

1 *Discount* Buy an accommodation bill in advance of the due date for less than the sum specified on the bill (the difference being equal to or greater than the related interest).

2 *money market* Dealers in short-term finance to whom the bill could be sold at a steep discount. Such bills could change hands a number of times so that the party signing the bill might finally have to settle the debt with an unknown and unaccommodating party.

3 *table-beer* Beer of low alcoholic content.

request that I would read it at my leisure. I also took the opportunity of my holding a candle over the bannisters to light them down, when Mr. Micawber was going first, leading Mrs. Micawber, to detain Traddles for a moment on the top of the stairs.

"Traddles, Mr. Micawber don't mean any harm, but, if I were you, I wouldn't lend him anything."

"My dear Copperfield, I haven't got anything to lend."

"You have got a name, you know."

"Oh, you call *that* something to lend?"

"Certainly."

"Oh, yes, to be sure! I am very much obliged to you, Copperfield, but—I am afraid I have lent him that already."

"For the bill that is to go into the money market?"

"No, not for that one. This is the first I have heard of that one. I have been thinking that he will most likely propose that one on the way home. Mine's another."

"I hope there will be nothing wrong about it."

"I hope not. I should think not, though, because he told me, only the other day, that it was provided for. That was Mr. Micawber's expression, 'provided for'."

Mr. Micawber looking up at this juncture, I had only time to repeat my caution. Traddles thanked me, and descended. But I was much afraid, when I observed the good-natured manner in which he went down with Mrs. Micawber's cap in his hand, that he would be carried into the money market, neck and heels.[1]

I returned to my fireside, and read Mr. Micawber's letter, which was dated an hour and a half before dinner. I am not sure whether I have mentioned that, when Mr. Micawber was at any particularly desperate crisis, he used a sort of legal phraseology, which he seemed to think equivalent to winding up his affairs.

This was the letter.

Sir—for I dare not say my dear Copperfield—It is expedient that I should inform you that the undersigned is Crushed. Some flickering efforts to spare the premature knowledge of his calamitous position, you may observe in him this day; but hope has sunk beneath the horizon, and the undersigned is Crushed.

---

1   *neck and heels* Entirely.

The present communication is penned within the personal range (I cannot call it the society) of an individual in a state closely bordering on intoxication, employed by a broker. That individual is in legal possession of the premises, under a distress for rent. His inventory includes, not only the chattels and effects of every description belonging to the undersigned, as yearly tenant of this habitation, but also those appertaining to Mr. Thomas Traddles, lodger, a member of the Honourable Society of the Inner Temple.[1]

If any drop of gloom were wanting in the overflowing cup, which is now 'commended' (in the language of an immortal Writer) to the lips of the undersigned,[2] it would be found in the fact that a friendly acceptance granted to the undersigned by the before-mentioned Mr. Thomas Traddles, for the sum of £23 4s. 9½d.,[3] is overdue, and is not provided for. Also, in the fact, that the living responsibilities clinging to the undersigned will, in the course of nature, be increased by the sum of one more helpless victim, whose miserable appearance may be looked for—in round numbers—at the expiration of a period not exceeding six lunar months from the present date.

After premising thus much, it would be a work of supererogation to add that dust and ashes are forever scattered

On

The

Head

Of

WILKINS MICAWBER.

CHAPTER 4

Seldom did I wake at night, seldom did I look up at the moon, or stars, or watch the falling rain, or hear the wind, but I thought of the solitary figure of the good fisherman, toiling on—poor Pilgrim—and

---

1 *Honourable Society of the Inner Temple* Professional association of lawyers.

2 *If any ... the undersigned* Cf. Shakespeare's *Macbeth* 1.7.10–12: "This even-handed justice / Commends the ingredients of our poisoned chalice / To our own lips."

3 *£23 4s. 9½d.* Twenty-three pounds, four shillings, nine and a half pence.

recalled his words, "I'm a going to seek my niece. I'm a going to seek her fur and wide."

Months passed, and he had been absent—no one knew where—the whole time. It had been a bitter day in London, and a cutting northeast wind had blown. The wind had gone down with the light, and snow had come on. My shortest way home—and I naturally took the shortest way on such a night—was through Saint Martin's Lane. On the steps of the church there was the figure of a man, and I stood face to face with Mr. Peggotty.

"Mas'r Davy! It do my art good to see you, sir. Well met, well met!"

"Well met, my dear old friend!"

"I had thowts o' coming to make inquiration for you, sir, to-night, but it was too late. I should have come early in the morning, sir, afore going away agen."

"Again?"

"Yes, sir, I'm away to-morrow."

In those days there was a side entrance to the stable-yard of the Golden Cross Inn. Two or three public-rooms opened out of the yard, and looking into one of them, and finding it empty and a good fire burning, I took him in there.

"I'll tell you, Mas'r Davy, wheer-all I've been, and what-all we've heerd. I've been fur, and we've heerd little; but I'll tell you."

As he sat thinking, there was a fine massive gravity in his face which I did not venture to disturb.

"You see, sir, when she was a child she used to talk to me a deal about the sea, and about them coasts where the sea got to be dark blue, and to lay a shining and a shining in the sun. When she was lost, I know'd in my mind as he would take her to them countries. I know'd in my mind as he'd have told her wonders of 'em, and how she was to be a lady theer, and how he first got her to listen to him along o' sech like. I went across channel to France, and landed theer, as if I'd fell down from the skies. I found out a English gentleman, as was in authority, and told him I was going to seek my niece. He got me them papers as I wanted fur to carry me through—I doen't rightly know how they're called—and he would have give me money, but that I was thankful to have no need on. I thank him kind for all he done, I'm sure. I told him, best as I was able, what my gratitoode was, and went away through France, fur to seek my niece."

"Alone, and on foot?"

"Mostly afoot; sometimes in carts, along with people going to market; sometimes in empty coaches. Many mile a day afoot, and often with some poor soldier or another, travelling fur to see his friends. I couldn't talk to him, nor he to me; but we was company for one another, too, along the dusty roads. When I come to any town, I found the inn, and waited about the yard till some one came by (some one mostly did) as know'd English. Then I told how that I was on my way to seek my niece, and they told me what manner of gentlefolks was in the house, and I waited to see any as seemed like her, going in or out. When it warn't Em'ly, I went on agen. By little and little, when I come to a new village or that, among the poor people, I found they know'd about me. They would set me down at their cottage doors, and give me what-not fur to eat and drink, and show me where to sleep. And many a woman, Mas'r Davy, as has had a daughter about Em'ly's age, I've found a-waiting for me, at Our Saviour's Cross outside the village, fur to do me sim'lar kindnesses. Some has had daughters as was dead. And God only knows how good them mothers was to me!"

I laid my trembling hand upon the hand he put before his face. "Thank'ee, sir, doen't take no notice.

"At last I come to the sea. It warn't hard, you may suppose, for a seafaring man like me to work his way over to Italy. When I got theer I wandered on as I had done afore. I got news of her being seen among them Swiss mountains yonder. I made for them mountains, day and night. Ever so fur as I went, ever so fur them mountains seemed to shift away from me. But I come up with 'em, and I crossed 'em. I never doubted her. No! Not a bit! On'y let her see my face—on'y let her heer my voice—on'y let my stanning still afore her bring to her thoughts the home she had fled away from, and the child she had been—and if she had growed to be a royal lady, she'd have fell down at my feet! I know'd it well! I bought a country dress to put upon her. To put that dress upon her, and to cast off what she wore—to take her on my arm again, and wander towards home—to stop sometimes upon the road and heal her bruised feet and her worse bruised heart—was all I thowt of now. But, Mas'r Davy, it warn't to be—not yet! I was too late, and they was gone. Wheer, I couldn't learn. Some said heer, some said theer. I travelled heer, and I travelled theer, but I found no Em'ly, and I travelled home."

"How long ago?"

"A matter o' fower days. I sighted the old boat arter dark, and I never could have thowt, I'm sure, that the old boat would have been so strange."

From some pocket in his breast he took out, with a very careful hand, a small paper bundle containing two or three letters or little packets which he laid upon the table.

"The faithful creetur Mrs. Gummidge gave me these. This first one come afore I had been gone a week. A fifty pound bank-note in a sheet of paper, directed to me, and put underneath the door in the night. She tried to hide her writing, but she couldn't hide it from Me! This one come to Missis Gummidge two or three months ago. Five pounds."

It was untouched, like the previous sum, and he refolded both.

"Is that another letter in your hand?"

"It's money too, sir. Ten pound, you see. And wrote inside, 'From a true friend.' But the two first was put underneath the door, and this come by the post, day afore yesterday. I'm going to seek her at the post-mark."

He showed it to me. It was a town on the Upper Rhine. He had found out at Yarmouth some foreign dealers who knew that country, and they had drawn him a rude[1] map on paper, which he could very well understand.

I asked him how Ham was.

"He works as bold as a man can. He's never been heerd fur to complain. But my belief is ('twixt ourselves), as it has cut him deep. Well! Having seen you to-night, Mas'r Davy (and that does me good), I shall away betimes[2] to-morrow morning. You have seen what I've got heer," putting his hand on where the little packet lay. "All that troubles me is, to think that any harm might come to me afore this money was give back. If I was to die, and it was lost or stole or else-ways made away with, and it was never know'd by him but what I'd accepted of it, I believe the tother wureld wouldn't hold me! I believe I must come back!"

He rose, and I rose too. We grasped each other by the hand again; and as we went out into the rigorous night, everything seemed to be

---

1 *rude* Crude or simple.
2 *betimes* Early.

hushed in reverence for him, when he resumed his solitary journey through the snow.

CHAPTER 5

All this time I had gone on loving Dora harder than ever. If I may so express it, I was steeped in Dora. I was not merely over head and ears in love with her, I was saturated through and through. I took night walks to Norwood[1] where she lived, and perambulated round and round the house and garden for hours together, looking through crevices in the palings, using violent exertions to get my chin above the rusty nails on the top, blowing kisses at the lights in the windows, and romantically calling on the night to shield my Dora—I don't exactly know from what—I suppose from fire, perhaps from mice, to which she had a great objection.

Dora had a discreet friend, comparatively stricken in years, almost of the ripe age of twenty, I should say, whose name was Miss Mills. Dora called her Julia. She was the bosom friend of Dora. Happy Miss Mills!

One day Miss Mills said: "Dora is coming to stay with me. She is coming the day after to-morrow. If you would like to call, I am sure papa would be happy to see you."

I passed three days in a luxury of wretchedness. At last, arrayed for the purpose, at a vast expense, I went to Miss Mills's, fraught with a declaration.

Mr. Mills was not at home. I didn't expect he would be. Nobody wanted *him*. Miss Mills was at home. Miss Mills would do.

I was shown into a room up stairs, where Miss Mills and Dora were. Dora's little dog Jip was there. Miss Mills was copying music, and Dora was painting flowers. What were my feelings when I recognized flowers I had given her!

Miss Mills was very glad to see me, and very sorry her papa was not at home, though I thought we all bore that with fortitude. Miss Mills was conversational for a few minutes, and then, laying down her pen, got up and left the room.

---

1 *Norwood* Part of Lambeth, in south London.

I began to think I would put it off till to-morrow.

"I hope your poor horse was not tired when he got home at night from that picnic," said Dora, lifting up her beautiful eyes. "It was a long way for him."

I began to think I would do it to-day.

"It was a long way for *him*, for *he* had nothing to uphold him on the journey."

"Wasn't he fed, poor thing? asked Dora.

I began to think I would put it off till to-morrow.

"Ye—yes, he was well taken care of. I mean he had not the unutterable happiness that I had in being so near you."

I saw now that I was in for it, and it must be done on the spot.

"I don't know why you should care for being near me," said Dora, "or why you should call it a happiness. But of course you don't mean what you say. Jip, you naughty boy, come here!"

I don't know how I did it, but I did it in a moment. I intercepted Jip. I had Dora in my arms. I was full of eloquence. I never stopped for a word. I told her how I loved her. I told her I should die without her. I told her that I idolized and worshipped her. Jip barked madly all the time. My eloquence increased, and I said, if she would like me to die for her, she had but to say the word, and I was ready. I had loved her to distraction every minute, day and night, since I first set eyes upon her. I loved her at that minute to distraction. I should always love her, every minute, to distraction. Lovers had loved before, and lovers would love again; but no lover had ever loved, might, could, would, or should ever love, as I loved Dora. The more I raved, the more Jip barked. Each of us in his own way got more mad every moment.

Well, well! Dora and I were sitting on the sofa by and by, quiet enough, and Jip was lying in her lap, winking peacefully at me. It was off my mind. I was in a state of perfect rapture. Dora and I were engaged.

Being poor, I felt it necessary the next time I went to my darling to expatiate on that unfortunate drawback. I soon carried desolation into the bosom of our joys—not that I meant to do it, but that I was so full of the subject—by asking Dora, without the smallest preparation, if she could love a beggar.

"How can you ask me anything so foolish? Love a beggar!"

"Dora, my own dearest, I am a beggar!"

"How can you be such a silly thing," replied Dora, slapping my hand, "as to sit there, telling such stories? I'll make Jip bite you, if you are so ridiculous."

But I looked so serious that Dora began to cry. She did nothing but exclaim, Oh dear! Oh dear! And oh, she was so frightened! And where was Julia Mills! And oh, take her to Julia Mills, and go away, please! until I was almost beside myself.

I thought I had killed her. I sprinkled water on her face; I went down on my knees; I plucked at my hair; I implored her forgiveness; I besought her to look up; I ravaged Miss Mills's work-box for a smelling-bottle,[1] and, in my agony of mind, applied an ivory needle-case instead, and dropped all the needles over Dora.

At last I got Dora to look at me, with a horrified expression which I gradually soothed until it was only loving, and her soft, pretty cheek was lying against mine.

"Is your heart mine still, dear Dora?"

"Oh yes! Oh yes! it's all yours. Oh, don't be dreadful!"

"My dearest love, the crust well earned—"

"Oh yes; but I don't want to hear any more about crusts. And after we are married, Jip must have a mutton-chop every day at twelve, or he'll die."

I was charmed with her childish, winning way, and I fondly explained to her that Jip should have his mutton-chop with his accustomed regularity.

When we had been engaged some half-year or so, Dora delighted me by asking me to give her that cookery-book I had once spoken of, and to show her how to keep accounts, as I had once promised I would. I brought the volume with me on my next visit (I got it prettily bound, first, to make it look less dry and more inviting), and showed her an old housekeeping book of my aunt's, and gave her a set of tablets, and a pretty little pencil-case, and a box of leads, to practise house-keeping with.

But the cookery-book made Dora's head ache, and the figures made her cry. They wouldn't add up, she said. So she rubbed them

---

1   *smelling-bottle* Bottle of smelling salts, used to revive a person who has fainted.

out, and drew little nosegays, and likenesses of me and Jip, all over the tablets.

Time went on, and at last, here in this hand of mine, I held the wedding licence. There were the two names in the sweet old visionary connection—David Copperfield and Dora Spenlow; and there in the corner was that parental Institution, the Stamp Office, looking down upon our union; and there, in the printed form of words, was the Archbishop of Canterbury, invoking a blessing on us, and doing it as cheap as could possibly be expected.

I doubt whether two young birds could have known less about keeping house than I and my pretty Dora did. We had a servant, of course. *She* kept house for us. We had an awful time of it with Mary Anne.

Her name was Paragon. Her nature was represented to us, when we engaged her, as being feebly expressed in her name. She had a written character,[1] as large as a Proclamation, and according to this document could do everything of a domestic nature that ever I heard of, and a great many things that I never did hear of. She was a woman in the prime of life; of a severe countenance, and subject (particularly in the arms) to a sort of perpetual measles. She had a cousin in the Life Guards,[2] with such long legs that he looked like the afternoon shadow of somebody else. She was warranted sober and honest; and I am therefore willing to believe that she was in a fit when we found her under the boiler, and that the deficient teaspoons were attributable to the dustman.[3] She was the cause of our first little quarrel.

"My dearest life," I said one day to Dora, "do you think Mary Anne has any idea of time?"

"Why, Doady?"

"My love, because it's five, and we were to have dined at four."

My little wife came and sat upon my knee, to coax me to be quiet, and drew a line with her pencil down the middle of my nose; but I couldn't dine off that, though it was very agreeable.

"Don't you think, my dear, it would be better for you to remonstrate with Mary Anne?"

---

1 *character* Letter of recommendation.
2 *Life Guards* Cavalry units charged with the task of guarding the royal family.
3 *dustman* Ashes from fireplace grates and other garbage were emptied into dustbins. Dustmen emptied the bins and sifted them for accidentally discarded valuables.

"Oh no, please! I couldn't, Doady!"

"Why not, my love?"

"Oh, because I am such a little goose, and she knows I am!"

I thought this sentiment so incompatible with the establishment of any system of check on Mary Anne, that I frowned a little.

"My precious wife, we must be serious sometimes. Come! sit down on this chair, close beside me! Give me the pencil! There! Now let us talk sensibly. You know, dear," what a little hand it was to hold, and what a tiny wedding-ring it was to see—"you know, my love, it is not exactly comfortable to have to go out without one's dinner. Now, is it?"

"N-n-no!" replied Dora, faintly.

"My love, how you tremble!"

"Because I know you're going to scold me."

"My sweet, I am only going to reason."

"Oh, but reasoning is worse than scolding! I didn't marry to be reasoned with. If you meant to reason with such a poor little thing as I am, you ought to have told me so, you cruel boy!"

"Dora, my darling!"

"No, I am not your darling. Because you *must* be sorry that you married me, or else you wouldn't reason with me!"

I felt so injured by the inconsequential nature of this charge, that it gave me courage to be grave.

"Now, my own Dora, you are childish, and are talking nonsense. You must remember, I am sure, that I was obliged to go out yesterday when dinner was half over; and that, the day before, I was made quite unwell by being obliged to eat underdone veal in a hurry; to-day, I don't dine at all, and I am afraid to say how long we waited for break-fast, and *then* the water didn't boil. I don't mean to reproach you, my dear, but this is not comfortable."

"Oh, you cruel, cruel boy, to say I am a disagreeable wife!"

"Now, my dear Dora, you must know that I never said that!"

"You said I wasn't comfortable!"

"I said the housekeeping was not comfortable."

"It's exactly the same thing! and I wonder, I do, at your making such ungrateful speeches. When you know that the other day, when you said you would like a little bit of fish, I went out myself, miles and miles, and ordered it to surprise you."

"And it was very kind of you, my own darling; and I felt it so much that I wouldn't, on any account, have mentioned that you bought a salmon, which was too much for two; or that it cost one pound six, which was more than we can afford."

"You enjoyed it very much," sobbed Dora. "And you said I was a Mouse."

"And I'll say so again, my love, a thousand times!"

I said it a thousand times, and more, and went on saying it until Mary Anne's cousin deserted into our coal-hole,[1] and was brought out, to our great amazement, by a piquet of his companions in arms, who took him away handcuffed in a procession that covered our front-garden with disgrace.

Everybody we had anything to do with seemed to cheat us. Our appearance in a shop was a signal for the damaged goods to be brought out immediately. If we bought a lobster it was full of water. All our meat turned out tough, and there was hardly any crust to our loaves.

As to the washerwoman pawning the clothes, and coming in a state of penitent intoxication to apologize, I suppose that might have happened several times to anybody. Also the chimney on fire, the parish engine, and perjury on the part of the beadle.[2] But I apprehend we were personally unfortunate in our page, whose principal function was to quarrel with the cook. We wanted to get rid of him, but he was very much attached to us, and wouldn't go, until one day he stole Dora's watch, and spent the produce (he was always a weak-minded boy) in riding up and down between London and Uxbridge[3] outside the coach.

He was taken to the Police Office on the completion of his fifteenth journey; when four-and-sixpence, and a second-hand fife which he couldn't play, were found upon his person.

He was tried, and ordered to be transported.[4] Even then he couldn't be quiet, but was always writing us letters; and he wanted so much to see Dora before he went away, that Dora went to visit him, and fainted when she found herself inside the iron bars. I had no peace of my life

---

1 *deserted into our coal-hole* I.e., deserted from the Life Guards and hid in the Copperfields' coal cellar.

2 *engine* Fire engine; *beadle* Low-ranking parish official.

3 *Uxbridge* Town just west of London.

4 *transported* Sent to a colony, probably in Australia, to serve his sentence.

until he was expatriated and made (as I afterwards heard) a shepherd of "up the country" somewhere, I have no geographical idea where.

"I am very sorry for all this, Doady," said Dora. "Will you call me a name I want you to call me?"

"What is it, my dear?"

"It's a stupid name—Child-wife. When you are going to be angry with me, say to yourself 'It's only my Child-wife.' When I am very disappointing, say, 'I knew a long time ago, that she would make but a Child-wife.' When you miss what you would like me to be, and what I should like to be, and what I think I never can be, say, 'Still my foolish Child-wife loves me.' For indeed I do."

I invoke the innocent figure that I dearly loved to come out of the mists and shadows of the past, and to turn its gentle head towards me once again, and to bear witness that it was made happy by what I answered. ·

Chapter 6

I heard a footstep on the stairs one day. I knew it to be Mr. Peggotty's. It came nearer, nearer, rushed into the room.

"Mas'r Davy, I've found her! I thank my Heavenly Father for having guided of me in his own ways to my darling!"

"You have made up your mind as to the future, good friend?"

"Yes, Mas'r Davy, theer's mighty countries fur from heer. Our future life lays over the sea."

As he gave me both his hands, hurrying to return to the one charge of his noble existence, I thought of Ham, and who would break the intelligence to him. Mr. Peggotty thought of everything. He had already written to the poor fellow, and had the letter in the pocket of his rough coat, ready for the post. I asked him for it, and said I would go down to Yarmouth, and talk to Ham myself before I gave it him, and prepare him for its contents. He thanked me very earnestly, and we parted, with the understanding that I would go down by the mail[1] that same night. In the evening I started.

---

1 *by the mail* Mail coaches could carry one or two additional passengers on the outside and were used if quick transportation was required.

"Don't you think that," I asked the coachman, in the first stage out of London, "a very remarkable sky? I don't remember to have ever seen one like it."

"Nor I. That's wind, sir. There'll be mischief done at sea before long."

It was a murky confusion of flying clouds tossed up into most remarkable heaps, through which the wild moon seemed to plunge headlong, as if, in a dread disturbance of the laws of nature, she had lost her way. There had been a wind all day; and it was rising then, with an extraordinary great sound. In another hour it had much increased, and the sky was more overcast, and it blew hard.

But as the night advanced, it came on to blow harder and harder. Many times, in the dark part of the night (it was then late in September), we were in serious apprehension that the coach would be blown over; and when the day broke, the wind blew harder, and still harder. I had been in Yarmouth when the seamen said it blew great guns, but I had never known the like of this, or anything approaching to it.

As we struggled on, nearer and nearer to the sea, from which this mighty wind was blowing dead on shore, its force became more and more terrific. When we came within sight of the sea, the waves on the horizon, seen at intervals above the rolling abyss, were like glimpses of another shore with towers and buildings. When at last we got into the town, the people came out to their doors, making a wonder of the mail that had come through such a storm.

The tremendous sea itself, when I could find pause to look at it, in the agitation of the blinding wind, the flying stones and sand, and the awful noise, confounded me. As the high watery walls came rolling in, and tumbled into surf, I seemed to see a rending and upheaving of all nature.

Not finding Ham among the people whom this memorable wind—for it is still remembered down there as the greatest ever known to blow upon that coast—had brought together on the beach, I made my way to his house.

I learned that he had gone on a job of shipwright's work some miles away, but that he would be back to-morrow morning in good time.

So I went back to the inn; and when I had washed and dressed, and tried to sleep, but in vain, it was late in the afternoon. I had not sat five minutes by the coffee-room fire, when the waiter, coming to stir it, told me that two colliers had gone down, with all hands, a few miles off; and that some other ships had been seen labouring hard in the Roads,[1] and trying, in great distress, to keep off shore. Mercy on them, and on all poor sailors, said he, if we had another night like the last!

I could not eat, I could not sit still, I could not continue steadfast to anything. My dinner went away almost untasted, and I tried to refresh myself with a glass or two of wine. In vain. I walked to and fro, tried to read an old gazetteer,[2] listened to the awful noises, looked at faces, scenes, and figures in the fire. At length the ticking of the undisturbed clock on the wall tormented me to that degree that I resolved to go to bed.

For hours I lay in bed listening to the wind and water, imagining, now, that I heard shrieks out at sea; now, that I distinctly heard the firing of signal-guns; now, the fall of houses in the town. At length my restlessness attained to such a pitch that I hurried on my clothes and went down stairs. In the large kitchen all the inn servants and some other watchers were clustered together.

One man asked me, when I went in among them, whether I thought the souls of the collier's crews who had gone down were out in the storm.

I remained with these people, I dare say, two hours. Once I opened the yard gate and looked into the empty street. The sand, the sea-weed, and the flakes of foam were driving by, and I was obliged to call for assistance before I could shut the gate again, and make it fast against the wind.

There was a dark gloom in my lonely chamber, when I at length returned to it; but I was tired now, and, getting into bed again, fell into the depths of sleep until broad day; when I was aroused at eight or nine o'clock by some one knocking and calling at my door.

"What is the matter?"

"A wreck! close by!"

"What wreck?"

---

1 *the Roads* Stretch of water off the coast of Yarmouth.
2 *gazetteer* Newspaper.

"A schooner from Spain or Portugal, laden with fruit and wine. Make haste, sir, if you want to see her! It's thought down on the beach she'll go to pieces every moment."

I wrapped myself in my clothes as quickly as I could, and ran into the street, where numbers of people were before me, all running in one direction—to the beach. I ran the same way, outstripping a good many, and soon came facing the wild sea. Every appearance it had before presented bore the expression of being *swelled*; and the height to which the breakers rose and bore one another down, and rolled in, in interminable hosts, was most appalling.

In the difficulty of hearing anything but wind and waves, and in the crowd, and the unspeakable confusion, and my first breathless efforts to stand against the weather, I was so confused that I looked out to sea for the wreck, and saw nothing but the foaming heads of the great waves.

A boatman laid a hand upon my arm, and pointed. Then I saw it, close in upon us.

One mast was broken short off, six or eight feet from the deck, and lay over the side, entangled in a maze of sail and rigging; and all that ruin, as the ship rolled and beat—which she did with a violence quite inconceivable—beat the side as if it would stave it in. Some efforts were being made to cut this portion of the wreck away; for as the ship, which was broadside on, turned towards us in her rolling, I plainly descried her people at work with axes—especially one active figure, with long curling hair. But a great cry, audible even above the wind and water, rose from the shore; the sea, sweeping over the wreck, made a clean breach, and carried men, spars, casks, planks, bulwarks, heaps of such toys, into the boiling surge.

The second mast was yet standing, with the rags of a sail, and a wild confusion of broken cordage, flapping to and fro. The ship had struck once, the same boatman said, and then lifted in, and struck again. I understood him to add that she was parting amidships. As he spoke, there was another great cry of pity from the beach. Four men arose with the wreck out of the deep, clinging to the rigging of the remaining mast; uppermost, the active figure with the curling hair.

There was a bell on board; and as the ship rolled and dashed, this bell rang; and its sound, the knell of those unhappy men, was borne towards us on the wind. Again we lost her, and again she rose. Two of the four men were gone.

I noticed that some new sensation moved the people on the beach, and I saw them part, and Ham come breaking through them to the front.

Instantly I ran to him, for I divined that he meant to wade off with a rope. I held him back with both arms; and implored the men not to listen to him, not to let him stir that sand.

Another cry arose, and we saw the cruel sail, with blow on blow, beat off the lower of the two men, and fly up in triumph round the active figure left alone upon the mast. Against such a sight, and against such determination as that of the calmly desperate man, who was already accustomed to lead half the people present, I might as hopefully have entreated the wind.

I was swept away to some distance, where the people around me made me stay; urging, as I confusedly perceived, that he was bent on going, with help or without, and that I should endanger the precautions for his safety by troubling those with whom they rested. I saw hurry on the beach, and men running with ropes, and penetrating into a circle of figures that hid him from me. Then I saw him standing alone, in a seaman's frock and trousers, a rope in his hand, another round his body, and several of the best men holding to the latter.

The wreck was breaking up. I saw that she was parting in the middle, and that the life of the solitary man upon the mast hung by a thread. He had a singular red cap on, not like a sailor's cap, but of a finer colour; and as the few planks between him and destruction rolled and bulged, and as his death-knell rung, he was seen by all of us to wave this cap. I saw him do it now, and thought I was going distracted, when his action brought an old remembrance to my mind of a once dear friend, *the* once dear friend—Steerforth.

Ham watched the sea until there was a great retiring wave; when he dashed in after it, and in a moment was buffeting with the water, rising with the hills, falling with the valleys, lost beneath the foam— borne in towards the shore, borne on towards the ship.

At length he neared the wreck. He was so near, that with one more of his vigorous strokes he would be clinging to it, when, a high, green, vast hill-side of water moving on shoreward from beyond the ship, he seemed to leap up into it with a mighty bound—and the ship was gone!

They drew him to my very feet, insensible, dead. He was carried to the nearest house, and every means of restoration was tried; but he had been beaten to death by the great wave, and his generous heart was stilled forever.

As I sat beside the bed, when hope was abandoned, and all was done, a fisherman who had known me when Emily and I were children, and ever since, whispered my name at the door.

"Sir, will you come over yonder?"

The old remembrance that had been recalled to me was in his look, and I asked him, "Has a body come ashore?"

"Yes."

"Do I know it?"

He answered nothing. But he led me to the shore. And on that part of it where she and I had looked for shells, two children—on that part of it where some lighter fragments of the old boat blown down last night had been scattered by the wind—among the ruins of the home he had wronged—I saw him lying with his head upon his arm, as I had often seen him lie at school.

—1861

Sikes and Nancy

CHAPTER I

Fagin the receiver of stolen goods was up, betimes,[1] one morning, and waited impatiently for the appearance of his new associate, Noah Claypole, otherwise[2] Morris Bolter; who at length presented himself, and, cutting a monstrous slice of bread, commenced a voracious assault on the breakfast.

"Bolter, Bolter."

"Well, here I am. What's the matter? Don't yer ask me to do anything till I have done eating. That's a great fault in this place. Yer never get time enough over yer meals."

"You can talk as you eat, can't you?"

"Oh yes, I can talk. I get on better when I talk. Talk away. Yer won't interrupt me."

There seemed, indeed, no great fear of anything interrupting him, as he had evidently sat down with a determination to do a deal of business.

"I want you, Bolter," leaning over the table, "to do a piece of work for me, my dear, that needs great care and caution."

"I say, don't yer go a-shoving me into danger, yer know. That don't suit me, that don't; and so I tell yer."

"There's not the smallest danger in it—not the very smallest; it's only to dodge[3] a woman."

"An old woman?"

"A young one."

"I can do that pretty well. I was a regular sneak when I was at school. What am I to dodge her for? Not to—"

"Not to do anything, but tell me where she goes, who she sees, and, if possible, what she says; to remember the street, if it is a street, or the house, if it is a house; and to bring me back all the information you can."

---

1 *betimes* Early.
2 *otherwise* Also known as; "Morris Bolter" is an alias.
3 *dodge* Follow.

"What'll yer give me?"

"If you do it well, a pound, my dear. One pound. And that's what I never gave yet, for any job of work where there wasn't valuable consideration to be got."

"Who is she?"

"One of us."

"Oh Lor! Yer doubtful of her, are yer?"

"She has found out some new friends, my dear, and I must know who they are."

"I see. Ha! ha! ha! I'm your man. Where is she? Where am I to wait for her? Where am I to go?"

"All that, my dear, you shall hear from me. I'll point her out at the proper time. You keep ready, in the clothes I have got here for you, and leave the rest to me."

That night, and the next, and the next again, the spy sat booted and equipped in the disguise of a carter:[1] ready to turn out at a word from Fagin. Six nights passed, and on each, Fagin came home with a disappointed face, and briefly intimated that it was not yet time. On the seventh he returned exultant. It was Sunday Night.

"She goes abroad tonight," said Fagin, "and on the right errand, I'm sure; for she has been alone all day, and the man she is afraid of will not be back much before daybreak. Come with me! Quick!"

They left the house, and, stealing through a labyrinth of streets, arrived at length before a public-house. It was past eleven o'clock, and the door was closed; but it opened softly as Fagin gave a low whistle. They entered, without noise.

Scarcely venturing to whisper, but substituting dumb show for words, Fagin pointed out a pane of glass high in the wall to Noah, and signed to him to climb up, on a piece of furniture below it, and observe the person in the adjoining room.

"Is that the woman?"

Fagin nodded "yes."

"I can't see her face well. She is looking down, and the candle is behind her."

"Stay there." He signed to the lad, who had opened the house-door to them; who withdrew—entered the room adjoining, and, under

---

1 *carter* Cart driver.

pretence of snuffing the candle, moved it in the required position; then he spoke to the girl, causing her to raise her face.

"I see her now!"

"Plainly?"

"I should know her among a thousand."

The spy descended, the room-door opened, and the girl came out. Fagin drew him behind a small partition, and they held their breath as she passed within a few feet of their place of concealment, and emerged by the door at which they had entered.

"After her!! To the left. Take the left hand, and keep on the other side. After her!!"

The spy darted off; and, by the light of the street lamps, saw the girl's retreating figure, already at some distance before him. He advanced as near as he considered prudent, and kept on the opposite side of the street. She looked nervously round. She seemed to gather courage as she advanced, and to walk with a steadier and firmer step. The spy preserved the same relative distance between them, and followed.

CHAPTER 2

The churches chimed three quarters past eleven, as the two figures emerged on London Bridge. The young woman advanced with a swift and rapid step, and looked about her as though in quest of some expected object; the young man, who slunk along in the deepest shadow he could find, and, at some distance, accommodated his pace to hers: stopping when she stopped: and as she moved again, creeping stealthily on: but never allowing himself, in the ardour of his pursuit, to gain upon her. Thus, they crossed the bridge, from the Middlesex to the Surrey shore, when the woman, disappointed in her anxious scrutiny of the foot-passengers, turned back. The movement was sudden; but the man was not thrown off his guard by it; for, shrinking into one of the recesses which surmount the piers of the bridge, and leaning over the parapet the better to conceal his figure, he suffered her to pass. When she was about the same distance in advance as she had been before, he slipped quietly down, and followed her again. At nearly the centre of the bridge she stopped. He stopped.

It was a very dark night. The day had been unfavourable, and at that hour and place there were few people stirring. Such as there were, hurried past: possibly without seeing, certainly without noticing, either the woman, or the man. Their appearance was not attractive of such of London's destitute population, as chanced to take their way over the bridge that night; and they stood there in silence: neither speaking nor spoken to.

The girl had taken a few turns to and fro—closely watched by her hidden observer—when the heavy bell of St. Paul's tolled for the death of another day. Midnight had come upon the crowded city. Upon the palace, the night-cellar, the jail, the madhouse: the chambers of birth and death, of health and sickness, upon the rigid face of the corpse and the calm sleep of the child.

A young lady, accompanied by a grey-haired gentleman, alighted from a hackney-carriage.[1] They had scarcely set foot upon the pavement of the bridge, when the girl started, and joined them.

"Not here!! I am afraid to speak to you here. Come away—out of the public road—down the steps yonder!"

The steps to which she pointed were those which, on the Surrey bank, and on the same side of the bridge as Saint Saviour's Church, form a landing-stairs from the river. To this spot the spy hastened unobserved; and after a moment's survey of the place, he began to descend.

These stairs are a part of the bridge; they consist of three flights. Just below the end of the second, going down, the stone wall on the left terminates in an ornamental pilaster[2] facing towards the Thames. At this point the lower steps widen: so that a person turning that angle of the wall is necessarily unseen by any others on the stairs who chance to be above, if only a step. The spy looked hastily round, when he reached this point; and as there seemed no better place of concealment, and as the tide being out there was plenty of room, he slipped aside, with his back to the pilaster; and there waited: pretty certain that they would come no lower down.

So tardily went the time in this lonely place, and so eager was the spy, that he was on the point of emerging from his hiding-place, and

---

1 *hackney-carriage* Four-wheeled, private carriage—an elegant mode of transportation.
2 *pilaster* Column.

regaining the road above, when he heard the sound of footsteps, and directly afterwards of voices almost close at his ear.

He drew himself straight upright against the wall, and listened attentively.

"This is far enough," said a voice, which was evidently that of the gentleman. "I will not suffer the young lady to go any further. Many people would have distrusted you too much to have come even so far, but you see I am willing to humour you."

"To humour me!" cried the voice of the girl whom he had followed. "You're considerate, indeed, sir. To humour me! Well, well, it's no matter."

"Why, for what purpose can you have brought us to this strange place? Why not have let me speak to you, above there, where it is light, and there is something stirring, instead of bringing us to this dark and dismal hole?"

"I told you before that I was afraid to speak to you there. I don't know why it is," said the girl shuddering, "but I have such a fear and dread upon me tonight that I can hardly stand."

"A fear of what?"

"I scarcely know of what—I wish I did. Horrible thoughts of death—and shrouds with blood upon them—and a fear that has made me burn as if I was on fire—have been upon me all day. I was reading a book tonight, to while the time away, and the same things came into the print."

"Imagination!"

"No imagination. I swear I saw "coffin" written in every page of the book in large black letters—aye, and they carried one close to me, in the streets tonight."

"There is nothing unusual in that. They have passed me often."

"*Real ones.* This was not."

"Pray speak to her kindly," said the young lady to the grey-haired gentleman. "Poor creature! She seems to need it."

"Bless you, miss, for that! Your haughty religious people would have held their heads up to see me as I am tonight, and would have preached of flames and vengeance. Oh, dear lady, why aren't those who claim to be God's own folks as gentle and as kind to us poor wretches as you!"

"You were not here last Sunday night, girl, as you appointed."

"I couldn't come. I was kept by force."

"By whom?"

"Bill—Sikes—him that I told the young lady of before."

"You were not suspected of holding any communication with anybody on the subject which has brought us here tonight, I hope?"

"No," replied the girl, shaking her head. "It's not very easy for me to leave him unless he knows why; I couldn't have seen the lady when I did, but that I gave him a drink of laudanum before I came away."

"Did he awake before you returned?"

"No; and neither he nor any of them suspect me."

"Good. Now listen to me. I am Mr. Brownlow, this young lady's friend. I wish you, in this young lady's interest, and for her sake, to deliver up Fagin."

"Fagin! I will not do it! I will never do it! Devil that he is, and worse than devil as he has been to me, as my teacher in all Devilry, I will never do it."

"Why?"

"For the reason that, bad life as he has led, I have led a bad life too; for the reason that there are many of us who have kept the same courses together, and I'll not turn upon them, who might—any of them—have turned upon me, but didn't, bad as they are. Last, for the reason—(how can I say it with the young lady here!)—that, among them, there is one—this Bill—this Sikes—the most desperate of all—that I can't leave. Whether it is God's wrath for the wrong I have done, I don't know, but I am drawn back to him through everything, and I should be, I believe, if I knew that I was to die by his hand!"

"But, put one man—not him—not one of the gang—the one man Monks into my hands, and leave him to me to deal with."

"What if he turns against the others?"

"I promise you that, in that case, there the matter shall rest; they shall go scot free."

"Have I the lady's promise for that?"

"You have," replied Rose Maylie, the young lady.

"I have been a liar, and among liars from a little child, but I will take your words."

After receiving an assurance from both that she might safely do so, she proceeded in a voice so low that it was often difficult for the listener to discover even the purport of what she said, to describe the means by which this one man Monks might be found and taken. But nothing would have induced her to compromise one of her own companions; little reason though she had, poor wretch! to spare them.

"Now," said the gentleman, when she had finished, "you have given us most valuable assistance, young woman, I wish you to be the better for it. What can I do to serve you?"

"Nothing."

"You will not persist in saying that; think now; take time. Tell me?"

"Nothing, sir. You can do nothing to help me. I am past all hope."

"You put yourself beyond the pale[1] of hope. The past has been a dreary waste with you, of youthful energies misspent, and such treasures lavished, as the Creator bestows but once and never grants again, but, for the future, you may hope! I do not say that it is in our power to offer you peace of heart and mind, for that must come as you seek it; but a quiet asylum, either in England, or, if you fear to remain here, in some foreign country, it is not only within the compass of our ability but our most anxious wish to secure you. Before the dawn of morning, before this river wakes to the first glimpse of daylight, you shall be placed as entirely beyond the reach of your former associates, and leave as complete an absence of all trace behind you, as if you were to disappear from the earth this moment.[2] Come! I would not have you go back to exchange one word with any old companion, or take one look at any old haunt. Quit them all, while there is time and opportunity!"

"She will be persuaded now," cried the young lady.

"I fear not, my dear."

"No, sir—no, miss. I am chained to my old life. I loathe and hate it, but I cannot leave it. When ladies as young and good, as happy and beautiful as you, miss, give away your hearts, love will carry even you all lengths. When such as I, who have no certain roof but the coffin-lid, and no friend in sickness or death but the hospital-nurse, set our rotten hearts on any man, who can hope to cure us!—This fear comes over me again. I must go home. Let us part. I shall be watched or seen. Go! Go! If I have done you any service, all I ask is, leave me, and let me go my way alone."

---

1 *pale* Boundary.

2 *I do not … this moment* Dickens deleted this passage from his later readings of this story.

"Take this purse," cried the young lady. "Take it for my sake, that you may have some resource in an hour of need and trouble."

"No! I have not done this for money. Let me have that to think of. And yet—give me something that you have worn—I should like to have something—no, no, not a ring, they'd rob me of that—your gloves or handkerchief—anything that I can keep, as having belonged to you. There. Bless you! God bless you!! Goodnight, goodnight!"

The agitation of the girl, and the apprehension of some discovery which would subject her to violence, seemed to determine the gentleman to leave her. The sound of retreating footsteps followed, and the voices ceased.

After a time Nancy ascended to the street. The spy remained on his post for some minutes, and then, after peeping out to make sure that he was unobserved, darted away, and made for Fagin's house as fast as his legs would carry him.

CHAPTER 3

It was nearly two hours before daybreak; that time which in the autumn of the year may be truly called the dead of night; when the streets are silent and deserted; when even sound appears to slumber, and profligacy and riot[1] have staggered home to dream; it was at this still and silent hour that Fagin sat in his old lair. Stretched upon a mattress on the floor lay Noah Claypole, otherwise Morris Bolter, fast asleep. Towards him the old man sometimes directed his eyes for an instant, and then brought them back again to the wasting candle.

He sat without changing his attitude, or appearing to take the smallest heed of time, until the doorbell rang. He crept upstairs, and presently returned accompanied by a man muffled to the chin, who carried a bundle under one arm. Throwing back his outer coat, the man displayed the burly frame of Sikes, the housebreaker.

"There!" laying the bundle on the table. "Take care of that, and do the most you can with it. It's been trouble enough to get. I thought I should have been here three hours ago."

---

1   *profligacy and riot* Debauchery and rowdiness.

Fagin laid his hand upon the bundle, and locked it in the cupboard. But he did not take his eyes off the robber, for an instant.

"Wot now?" cried Sikes. "Wot do you look at a man, like that, for?"

Fagin raised his right hand, and shook his trembling forefinger in the air.

"Hallo!" feeling in his breast. "He's gone mad. I must look to myself here."

"No, no, it's not—you're not the person, Bill. I've no—no fault to find with you."

"Oh! you haven't, haven't you?" passing a pistol into a more convenient pocket. "That's lucky—for one of us. Which one that is, don't matter."

"I've got that to tell you, Bill, will make you worse than me."

"Aye? Tell away! Look sharp, or Nance will think I'm lost."

"Lost! She has pretty well settled that, in her own mind, already."

He looked, perplexed, into the old man's face, and reading no satisfactory explanation of the riddle there, clenched his coat collar in his huge hand and shook him soundly.

"Speak, will you? Or if you don't, it shall be for want of breath. Open your mouth and say wot you've got to say. Out with it, you thundering, blundering, wondering old cur, out with it!"

"Suppose that lad that's lying there—" Fagin began.

Sikes turned round to where Noah was sleeping, as if he had not previously observed him. "Well?"

"Suppose that lad was to peach[1]—to blow upon us all. Suppose that lad was to do it, of his own fancy—not grabbed, tried, earwigged[2] by the parson and brought to it on bread and water, but of his own fancy; to please his own taste; stealing out at nights to do it. Do you hear me? Suppose he did all this, what then?"

"What then? If he was left alive till I came, I'd grind his skull under the iron heel of my boot into as many grains as there are hairs upon his head."

"What if _I_ did it! _I_, that know so much, and could hang so many besides myself!"

---

1   _peach_ Betray; give evidence against.
2   _earwigged_ Persuaded secretly.

"I don't know. I'd do something in the jail that 'ud get me put in irons; and, if I was tried along with you, I'd fall upon you with them in the open court, and beat your brains out afore the people. I'd smash your head as if a loaded wagon had gone over it."

Fagin looked hard at the robber; and, motioning him to be silent, stooped over the bed upon the floor, and shook the sleeper to rouse him.

"Bolter! Bolter! Poor lad!" said Fagin, looking up with an expression of devilish anticipation, and speaking slowly and with marked emphasis.

"He's tired—tired with watching for *her* so long—watching for *her*, Bill."

"Wot d'ye mean?"

Fagin made no answer, but bending over the sleeper again, hauled him into a sitting posture. When his assumed name had been repeated several times, Noah rubbed his eyes, and, giving a heavy yawn, looked sleepily about him.

"Tell me that again—once again, just for him to hear," said the Jew, pointing to Sikes as he spoke.

"Tell yer what?" asked the sleepy Noah, shaking himself pettishly.

"That about—Nancy! You followed her?"

"Yes."

"To London Bridge?"

"Yes."

"Where she met two people?"

"So she did."

"A gentleman and a lady that she had gone to of her own accord before, who asked her to give up all her pals, and Monks first, which she did—and to describe him, which she did—and to tell her what house it was that we meet at, and go to, which she did—and where it could be best watched from, which she did—and what time the people went there, which she did. She did all this. She told it all, every word, without a threat, without a murmur—she did—did she not?"

"All right," replied Noah, scratching his head. "That's just what it was!"

"What did they say about last Sunday?"

"About last Sunday! Why, I told yer that before."

"Again. Tell it again!"

"They asked her," as he grew more wakeful, and seemed to have a dawning perception who Sikes was, "they asked her why she didn't come, last Sunday, as she promised. She said she couldn't."

"Why? Tell him that."

"Because she was forcibly kept at home by Bill—Sikes—the man that she had told them of before."

"What more of him? What more of Bill—Sikes—the man she had told him of before? Tell him that, tell him that."

"Why, that she couldn't very easily get out of doors unless he knew where she was going to, and so the first time she went to see the lady, she—ha! ha! ha! it made me laugh when she said it, that did—she gave him a drink of laudanum!! ha! ha! ha!"

Sikes rushed from the room, and darted up the stairs.

"Bill, Bill!" cried Fagin, following him, hastily. "A word. Only a word."

"Let me out. Don't speak to me! it's not safe. Let me out."

"Hear me speak a word," rejoined Fagin, laying his hand upon the lock. "You won't be—you won't be—too—violent, Bill?"

The day was breaking, and there was light enough for the men to see each other's faces. They exchanged a brief glance; there was the same fire in the eyes of both.

"I mean, not too—violent—for—for—safety. Be crafty, Bill, and not too bold."

The robber dashed into the silent streets.

Without one pause, or moment's consideration; without once turning his head to the right or left; without once raising his eyes to the sky, or lowering them to the ground, but looking straight before him with savage resolution: he muttered not a word, nor relaxed a muscle, until he reached his own house-door. He opened it softly, with a key; strode lightly up the stairs; and entering his own room, double-locked the door, and drew back the curtain of the bed.

The girl was lying, half-dressed, upon the bed. He had roused her from her sleep, for she raised herself with a hurried and startled look.

"Get up!"

"It *is* you, Bill!"

"Get up!!!"

There was a candle burning, but he drew it from the candlestick and hurled it under the grate. Seeing the faint light of early day without, the girl rose to undraw the curtain.

"Let it be. There's light enough for wot I've got to do."

"Bill, why do you look like that at me?"

The robber regarded her, for a few seconds, with dilated nostrils and heaving breast; then, grasping her by the head and throat, dragged her into the middle of the room, and placed his heavy hand upon her mouth.

"You were watched tonight, you she-devil; every word you said was heard."

"Then if every word I said was heard, it was heard that I spared you. Bill, dear Bill, you cannot have the heart to kill me. Oh! think of all I have given up, only this one night, for you. Bill, Bill! For dear God's sake, for your own, for mine, stop before you spill my blood!!! I have been true to you, upon my guilty soul I have!! The gentleman and that dear lady told me tonight of a home in some foreign country where I could end my days in solitude and peace. Let me see them again, and beg them on my knees, to show the same mercy to you; and let us both leave this dreadful place, and far apart lead better lives, and forget how we have lived, except in prayers, and never see each other more. It is never too late to repent. They told me so—I feel it now. But we must have time—we must have a little, little time!"

The housebreaker freed one arm, and grasped his pistol. The certainty of immediate detection if he fired flashed across his mind; and he beat it twice upon the upturned face that almost touched his own.

She staggered and fell, but raising herself on her knees, she drew from her bosom a white handkerchief—Rose Maylie's—and holding it up towards Heaven, breathed one prayer, for mercy to her Maker.

It was a ghastly figure to look upon. The murderer staggering backward to the wall, and shutting out the sight with his hand, seized a heavy club, and struck her down!!

The bright sun burst upon the crowded city in clear and radiant glory. Through costly-coloured glass and paper-mended window, through cathedral dome and rotten crevice, it shed its equal ray. It lighted up the room where the murdered woman lay. It did. He tried to shut it out, but it would stream in. If the sight had been a ghastly one in the dull morning, what was it, now, in all that brilliant light!!!

He had not moved; he had been afraid to stir. There had been a moan and motion of the hand; and, with terror added to rage, he had struck and struck again. Once he threw a rug over it; but it was worse to fancy the eyes, and imagine them moving towards him, than to see them glaring upward, as if watching the reflection of the pool of gore that quivered and danced in the sunlight on the ceiling. He had plucked it off again. And there was the body—mere flesh and blood, no more—but such flesh, and so much blood!!!

He struck a light, kindled a fire, and thrust the club into it. There was hair upon the end, which shrunk into a light cinder, and whirled up the chimney. Even that frightened him; but he held the weapon till it broke, and then piled it on the coals to burn away, and smoulder into ashes. He washed himself, and rubbed his clothes; there were spots upon them that would not be removed, but he cut the pieces out, and burnt them. How those stains were dispersed about the room! The very feet of his dog were bloody!!!

All this time he had, never once, turned his back upon the corpse. He now moved, backward, towards the door: dragging the dog with him, shut the door softly, locked it, took the key, and left the house.

As he gradually left the town behind him all that day, and plunged that night into the solitude and darkness of the country, he was haunted by that ghastly figure following at his heels. He could hear its garments rustle in the leaves; and every breath of wind came laden with that last low cry. If he stopped, it stopped. If he ran, it followed; not running too—that would have been a relief—but borne on one slow melancholy air that never rose or fell.

At times, he turned to beat this phantom off; though it should look him dead; but the hair rose on his head, and his blood stood still, for it had turned with him, and was behind him then. He leaned his back against a bank, and felt that it stood above him, visibly out against the cold night sky. He threw himself on his back upon the road. At his head it stood, silent, erect, and still: a human gravestone with its epitaph in blood!!

Suddenly, towards daybreak, he took the desperate resolution of going back to London. "There's somebody to speak to there, at all events. A hiding-place, too, in our gang's old house in Jacob's Island[1]—I'll risk it."

---

1   *Jacob's Island* Infamously squalid London slum. Located on the bank of the Thames, it was surrounded by waterways that during the Victorian era were essentially open sewers; the largest of these was Folly Ditch.

Choosing the least frequented roads for his journey back, he resolved to lie concealed within a short distance of the city until it was dark night again, and then proceed to his destination. He did this, and limped in among three affrighted fellow-thieves, the ghost of himself—blanched face, sunken eyes, hollow cheeks—his dog at his heels covered with mud, lame, half blind, crawling as if those stains had poisoned him!!

All three men shrank away. Not one of them spake.

"You that keep this house. Do you mean to sell me, or to let me lie here 'till the hunt is over?"

"You may stop if you think it safe. But what man ever escaped the men who are after you!"

Hark!!!! A great sound coming on like a rushing fire! What? Tracked so soon? The hunt was up already? Lights, gleaming below, voices in loud and earnest talk, hurried tramp of footsteps on the wooden bridges over Folly Ditch, a beating on the heavy door and window-shutters of the house, a waving crowd in the outer darkness like a field of corn moved by an angry storm!

"The tide was in, as I come up. Give me a rope. I may drop from the top of the house, at the back into the Folly Ditch, and clear off that way, or be stifled. Give me a rope!"

No one stirred. They pointed to where they kept such things, and the murderer hurried, with a strong cord to the housetop. Of all the terrific yells that ever fell on mortal ears, none could exceed the furious cry when he was seen. Some shouted to those who were nearest, to set the house on fire; others adjured the officers to shoot him dead; others, with execrations, clutched and tore at him in the empty air; some called for ladders, some for sledge-hammers; some ran with torches to and fro, to seek them. "I promise fifty pounds," cried Mr. Brownlow from the nearest bridge, "to the man who takes that murderer alive!"

He set his foot against the stack of chimneys, fastened one end of the rope firmly round it, and with the other made a strong running noose by the aid of his hands and teeth. With the cord round his back, he could let himself down to within a less distance of the ground than his own height, and had his knife ready in his hand to cut the cord, and drop.

At the instant that he brought the loop over his head before slipping it beneath his armpits, looking behind him on the roof he threw up his arms, and yelled, "The eyes again!" Staggering as if struck by lightning, he lost his balance and tumbled over the parapet. The noose was at his neck; it ran up with his weight; tight as a bowstring, and swift as the arrow it speeds. He fell five-and-thirty feet, and hung with his open knife clenched in his stiffening hand!!!

The dog which had lain concealed 'till now, ran backwards and forwards on the parapet with a dismal howl, and, collecting himself for a spring, jumped for the dead man's shoulders. Missing his aim, he fell into the ditch, turning over as he went, and striking against a stone, dashed out his brains!!

—1869

Anonymous, Dickens reading the murder of Nancy by Sikes.

In Context: The Readings of Charles Dickens

From Novel to Performance Fiction

To transform elements from his novels into pieces suited for performance, Dickens engaged in a thorough process of selection and revision. Usually, he physically cut and pasted passages from the original novel together and had them reprinted in larger, more easily readable text. He then altered these printed copies by hand, crossing out further cuts, adding rewritten material and performance directions in the margins, and sometimes even inserting whole pages of handwritten text.

The following selection—the opening of *Dombey and Son*—is included as an illustration of Dickens's approach to the content and wording of his performance fictions. The corresponding paragraphs from "The Story of Little Dombey" are reprinted on the facing page for ease of comparison.

from Charles Dickens, *Dombey and Son* (1846–48)

Dombey sat in the corner of the darkened room in the great arm-chair by the bedside, and Son lay tucked up warm in a little basket bedstead, carefully disposed on a low settee immediately in front of the fire and close to it, as if his constitution were analogous to that of a muffin, and it was essential to toast him brown while he was very new.

Dombey was about eight-and-forty years of age. Son about eight-and-forty minutes. Dombey was rather bald, rather red, and though a handsome well-made man, too stern and pompous in appearance to be prepossessing. Son was very bald, and very red, and though (of course) an undeniably fine infant, somewhat crushed and spotty in his general effect, as yet. On the brow of Dombey, Time and his brother Care had set some marks, as on a tree that was to come down in good time—remorseless twins they are for striding through their human forests, notching as they go—while the countenance of Son was crossed and recrossed with a thousand little creases, which the same deceitful Time would take delight in smoothing out and wear-ing away with the flat part of his scythe, as a preparation of the surface for his deeper operations.

Dombey, exulting in the long-looked-for event, jingled and jingled the heavy gold watch-chain that depended from below his trim blue coat, whereof the buttons sparkled phosphorescently in the feeble rays of the distant fire. Son, with his little fists curled up and clenched, seemed, in his feeble way, to be squaring at existence for having come upon him so unexpectedly. [...]

from Charles Dickens, "The Story of Little Dombey" (1858)

Rich Mr. Dombey sat in the corner of his wife's darkened bedchamber in the great arm-chair by the bedside, and rich Mr. Dombey's Son lay tucked up warm in a little basket, carefully placed on a low settee in front of the fire and close to it, as if his constitution were analogous to that of a muffin, and it was essential to toast him brown while he was very new.

Rich Mr. Dombey was about eight-and-forty years of age. Rich Mr. Dombey's Son, about eight-and-forty minutes. Mr. Dombey was rather bald, rather red, and rather stern and pompous. Mr. Dombey's son was very bald, and very red, and rather crushed and spotty in his general effect, as yet.

Mr. Dombey, exulting in the long-looked-for event, the birth of a son, jingled his heavy gold watch-chain as he sat in his blue coat and bright buttons by the side of the bed [...]

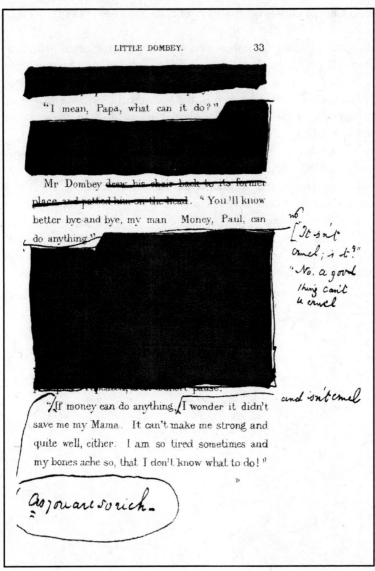

Page from Dickens's performance copy of "Little Dombey," 1858.

Reviews

Though Dickens attracted consistently large crowds for his readings, the reviews were somewhat more mixed. Many reviewers praised Dickens extravagantly, but a number of others concluded that he was much less accomplished as a performer than as a writer of fiction.

The following selection includes four reports from British and Irish newspapers of some of Dickens's early readings, together with three from American newspapers of Dickens on his triumphant tour of America in 1867–68. The report printed in the San Francisco *Alta California* is by Mark Twain, who was then 32 years old.

"Mr. Charles Dickens's Readings," *The Era* (13 June 1858)

The "Story of Little Dombey," which it is not too much to identify as one of the most touching episodes to be found in the works of any of our English novelists, was on Thursday night read at St. Martin's Hall, for the first time in public, by the author. There was a very full and highly fashionable attendance in that portion of the area set apart for the higher-priced visitors, but the great bulk of the public that had hitherto filled every corner of the galleries, either from counteracting attractions or from not readily understanding the time and place of this present reading, was to be sought for in vain. The peculiar circumstances under which Mr. Dickens made his bow to the audience, it being the first time he had appeared before the public since the publication of his letter denouncing and denying the scandalous stories that had been so cruelly circulated with respect to him,[1] gave a marked significance to the heartiness and cordial sympathy expressed in the rounds of applause accompanying his entrance on to the platform. Detaching from the story of "Dombey and Son" that earlier portion in which the premature intelligence and premature death of Little Dombey is so beautifully and so affectingly described, Mr. Dickens succeeded, even as we think, beyond his previous ef-

---

1 *The peculiar ... to him* In 1858, Dickens separated from his wife and was accused of conducting an extra-marital affair with an actress. He published a response in his defense on the front page of his magazine, *Household Words* (1850–59).

forts, in giving that remarkable vitality to his creations that enable us, for the first time, to hear the voice and see the figure of the speaker as well as to assist us in gathering our notions of his character from the words. It might safely be asserted, that out of the number that composed his audience, there was not one who did not feel that the pregnant meaning of many a passage was only then made known to him, and that the fullest conviction of the truthfulness to nature with which the characters had been drawn, resulted from the extraordinary dramatic powers with which these conceptions were realized. Dombey himself, "about eight-and-forty years of age, bald, rather red, and though a handsome, well-made man, too stern and pompous in his manner to be prepossessing," came vividly before us at the outset. The round, deep, sonorous voice of Dr. Parker Peps; the assiduous Mrs. Chick; the soft-voiced, spasmodically-admiring Miss Tox; the tune-humming Mr. John Chick; that wonderful Beadle, who invites the christening party to step into the vestry, and who seemed to start bodily out of the book for the purpose; the wheezy little pew-opener; the abrupt Mrs. Pipchin, the Brighton ogress; the portly Dr. Blimber, with that chin "so very double that it was a wonder how he ever managed to shave into the creases"; the Minerva-like Miss Blimber; the overgrown Toots, with his thick, chuckling tones, and kind purpose of expression; and the negus-exhilarated Mr. Feeder,[1] all passed in panoramic succession before the audience, not as abstract individualities, phantoms upraised by the magic of an ink-drop, but as living, moving, breathing personages that we had long known by name, but with whom for the first time we had here got on terms of intimacy. The exquisite pathos with which Mr. Dickens read that portion descriptive of the death of Little Dombey, and the touching love and faithfulness of his sister "Floy," brought tears into the eyes of his auditors, and they evidently felt it a relief at last to be able to conceal their half-suppressed emotions under a general round of thankful and most enthusiastic applause at the end. The reading terminated a little before ten o'clock, Mr. Dickens being once more called back to receive the tributes of his auditory in the double capacity of author and interpreter; and the impression left behind was one evidently cal-

---

1   *Dr. Parker Peps … Mr. Feeder* Characters in *Dombey and Son*, some of whom did not appear or were no longer mentioned by name in later revisions of the reading.

culated to raise the writer higher than ever in the esteem and affection of his numerous admirers.

from "Mr. Charles Dickens's Readings," *The Belfast News-Letter* (30 August 1858)

Mr. Charles Dickens gave his second and third readings on Saturday—the one at three o'clock in the afternoon, the other at eight o'clock in the evening. For the afternoon reading, the story of "Little Dombey" was selected. The attendance was numerous and highly respectable, and the arrangements were in all respects improved. There was no overcrowding, and the holders of reserved seat tickets obtained their proper places without difficulty.

Every reader of the works of Boz[1] is intimately acquainted with those chapters of "Dombey and Son" in which the story of Little Dombey is contained. The variety and the strongly-marked features of the characters represented afforded Mr. Dickens ample room for dramatic effect, and he was perfectly at home throughout. The solemn, stately Dombey, worshipping wealth, and demanding to be worshipped as its possessor; the aristocratic Dr. Parker Peps, the fulsome family surgeon; the ever-assuring Mrs. Chick; the ancient and unprotected Miss Tox; the infantine boardinghouse keeper, Mrs. Pipchin; the portly Dr. Blimber, "who only undertook the charge of ten young gentlemen," but had "a supply of learning for a hundred," and whose delight was to cram his unhappy decemvirate[2] with the full compliment of his knowledge; Miss Blimber, who was "dry and sandy with working in the graves of deceased languages—none of your live languages for Miss Blimber; they must be dead, stone dead, and then she dug them up like a ghoul"—Mrs. Blimber who affected to be so very learned that she said "if she could have known Cicero she thought she could have died contented," and who, at the great school ball, was "attired in such a number of skirts that it was quite an excursion to walk round her." All these were depicted with a truthfulness and humour that surpass description. The instantaneous change

---

1 *Boz* Early pen name of Charles Dickens.
2 *decemvirate* Latin: group of ten men.

of voice and manner were indeed most wonderful, considering the number and variety of the characters.

Mrs. Blimber's skirts, as a hit at a fashionable folly of our own time, were immensely applauded. But the inimitable Toots was an especial favourite with the audience, and caused not a little fun. The loving and charming Florence, whose devotion to her brother was ever so beautifully manifested; and the odd, old-fashioned, yet child-like little Dombey himself, were however the leading characters of the story; and many of the passages, which displayed the child in his "old, old moods" were read by the author in a manner peculiarly striking. [...]

The pathos with which the closing chapter was read drew tears from many eyes, and the solemn and beautiful concluding passage left upon the audience a mingled feeling of pain and pleasure. [...]

At the conclusion, Mr. Dickens was loudly applauded, and retired bowing his thanks to the house. The applause was continued for some time, but he did not return to the platform.

In the afternoon the Victoria Hall was crowded in every part, save that in the reserved seats a few places were vacant. Mr. Dickens, who was received with loud applause, prefaced the entertainment by requesting the audience to express freely any feeling which the stories might be so fortunate as to excite, and he complimented Belfast by stating that he had never the pleasure of addressing any audience more competent to appreciate the points of his narrative. He then proceeded to read "The Poor Traveller," "Boots at the Hollytree Inn,"[1] and "Mrs. Gamp." [...] "Sairy Gamp" was [...] the strong point of the evening. It was a little comedy in two chapters, in which all the characters were performed by the reader. The oily hypocrite, Picksniff [sic]; the piping imbecile, Chuffey; the voluble undertaker, Molds; and the inimitable Gamp herself, were distinct personations, and, as far as voice and accent were concerned, became distinct realities. The brief glimpse of Jonas Chuzzlewit gave an opportunity for the display of the highest dramatic power. The suspicious glance; the morose, churlish voice; the incessant biting of the thumb-nail, betrayed the conscious parricide. During the comic scenes, the irrepressible laugh-

---

1   *"The Poor Traveller"* Selection from "Seven Poor Travellers," printed in *Household Words* in 1854; *"Boots at the Hollytree Inn"* Selected from "The Holly-Tree Inn," printed in *Household Words* in 1855.

ter of the audience had free vent, and everyone present enjoyed a delightful evening.

We trust Mr. Dickens may find it convenient to pay us another visit next season.

from "Charles Dickens in Derby," *The Derby Mercury* (27 October 1858)

On Friday evening last, the Lecture Hall was filled to overflowing by a distinguished and fashionable assemblage who had gathered to welcome the most popular novelist of the day. The piece originally selected for Mr. Dickens' reading was the "Christmas Carol," but it was announced that "in compliance with what he believes to be a general wish," instead of this, "The Poor Traveller," "Boots at the Holly Tree Inn," and some chapters in the history of the notorious Mrs. Gamp would be read. We certainly think that Mr. Dickens was ill-advised in this change. The picturesque beauty and healthy tone of the "Christmas Carol" would have been infinitely preferable to the stereotypical vulgarity of "boots" and chamber-maids,[1] and the repulsive coarseness of Madames Gamp, Harris, and Betsey Prig. [...] [W]e must say that it was a breach of good taste—a needless and serious affront to ordinary refinement—to obtrude the gross remarks of these professional nurses on the ears of the young ladies who formed so large a portion of the audience: and it struck us that many of those present seemed half ashamed of the very partial laugh which these coarse jokes elicited. [...]

In ordinary lectures or readings, the journalist has nothing to do with the personal appearance of the Lecturer or Reader. He criticizes his performance, but not himself. In the case of Mr. Dickens, however, it is otherwise. Mr. Dickens comes to show himself, that is what people pay for, and Mr. Dickens, as his own showman, makes every provision that the public may enjoy a good stare at the lion. Mr. Dickens carries with him an artistically arranged apparatus for framing himself. The back-ground is of a well chosen brown, the carpet

---

1 *"boots" and chamber-maids*; Characters appearing in "Boots at the Holly Tree Inn";
   "boots" Hotel worker whose duties include shoe cleaning.

is green, the desk is green, and in front of Mr. Dickens are, not foot-lights, but face-lights, i.e. a line of gas jets, shielded from the audience by a drapery of the same brown colour, but throwing their light full on the face and person of the reader. When a man takes so much trouble to show himself, it can be no breach of propriety to try to describe him. Mr. Dickens is rather below than above the average height, and looks about five and forty. He has a considerable beard, and a good deal of moustache, which of course hides the mouth, and so conceals the play of one of the most expressive features. Mr. Dickens has a clear but not melodious voice, and his feigned voice "tells" with more effect in scraps of broad humour, such as proceed from "Mrs. Gamp" or "Boots," than in semi-poetical description.

On the whole we are inclined to doubt whether Mr. Dickens would refill the Lecture Hall on a second visit. We doubt whether there is sufficient intrinsic merit in the entertainment to attract, when you have satisfied the desire, so strong in the English mind, of see-ing for the first time any lion, whether literary, military, political, or quadruped.

For our own part, we confess that as admirers of many of Mr. Dickens's works—as appreciating the inimitable humour of "The Pickwick Papers," the touching pathos of the "Old Curiosity Shop," the photographic portraits of "Nicholas Nickleby" and "Oliver Twist"—we regret that their author should have been induced thus to make merchandise of himself, and to pander to one of the lowest tastes of the time, viz.,[1] the hunting after notabilities. [...] We are aware that another great week-day preacher, Mr. Thackeray,[2] has also read before public audiences; but he thought it worth while to write a course of admirable and brilliant lectures for the purpose: he did not read "a chapter from my published work." He did not frame himself for public inspection, nor did he affect to be an actor. Moreover, if he had, report says that he has the excuse of being poor, and poor by no fault of his own. Whereas report also says that if Mr. Dickens is not rich, never literary man had so golden opportunities. And we regret Mr. Dickens' exhibition also on this other ground, that he voluntarily

---

1 viz. Abbreviation for the Latin videlicet, meaning "that is to say."
2 Mr. Thackeray English novelist William Thackeray, whose success with his 1851 lecture series *English Humorists of the Eighteenth Century* encouraged Dickens to undertake his own public readings.

takes a lower place in the republic of letters than the world was ready to accord to him, when he stoops to court the suffrages of public favour among such rivals as Messrs. T.P. Barnum, Albert Smith, or Gordon Cumming.[1] We are free to confess the power of the temptation; for it is said, with what truth we know not, that Mr. Dickens cleared 300*l.* a-night by his readings in London, and perhaps half that sum in Derby and similar places, but we could wish that the prince of social photographers had not thus bowed himself down in the house of Mammon.[2] As we felt before we heard him at the Lecture Hall, so now we feel yet more strongly, that Mr. Dickens has seriously damaged the future of his reputation and influence, and that he has done what in him lay to lower the position of literary men in the social scale. [...]

"Mr. Charles Dickens," *The Times* (8 January 1859)

Never, probably, through the force of mere reading was a vast concourse held so completely within the grasp of one man as was the audience assembled in St. James's Hall to hear the episode of Nancy's murder from *Oliver Twist,* with which Mr. Charles Dickens has opened his second course of "farewell readings." As the tale of horror progressed, countenances became more and more fixed, and people listened with a sort of scared curiosity, which was all the more remarkable as nearly every one must have known what was coming as well as Mr. Dickens himself. Fagin and Noah Claypole, who, capitally impersonated, commence the story, caused now and then a little mirth, but directly Sikes made his appearance there was a general feeling that all must brace up their nerves to encounter something awful. Indeed, at the scene where the murder is actually committed, some ladies covered their faces with their hands, as if they would shut their

---

1 *T.P. Barnum* Showman T.P. Barnum (1810–91) was known for his freak shows and curiosity displays; he would begin his most famous venture, the Barnum and Bailey Circus, in 1881; *Albert Smith* Albert Richard Smith, a writer and mountain climber who performed a popular and extravagantly staged autobiographical entertainment entitled *The Ascent of Mont Blanc* (1852); *Gordon Cumming* Roulaeyn George Gordon-Cumming (1820–66), a big game hunter who lectured about his adventures in South Africa.
2 *Mammon* Personification of worldly wealth and greed.

eyes to horrors addressed to the imagination only. That in giving so potent a shock to the sensibilities of an assembly whose nerves may be considered more delicate than those of an average mass of playgoers there was something like peril Mr. Dickens was well aware. The question had arisen to his own mind whether, while striving to produce awe, he might not possibly cause disgust, and he did not venture to make his experiment with the general public till a chosen few had pronounced their judgment on the performance. The opinion of the select body that Nancy was to be publicly murdered without scruple has been more than confirmed by one of the largest audiences ever brought together by the force of Mr. Dickens' irresistible elocution.

The extracts from *Oliver Twist* are most judiciously made so as to include the whole story of the murder, with its antecedents and consequences, to the exclusion of all extraneous matter. First comes the dialogue, in which the Jew instructs Claypole to watch Nancy, then the interview of Nancy with Mr. Brownlow on London-bridge, then the scene where the Jew excites the wrath of Sikes by revealing the treachery of his mistress, then the murder itself, and, lastly, the death of the murderer.

It is in the scene where the crime is committed that Mr. Dickens displays his force to the utmost, and nothing can be more impressive than the despairing entreaties of the unfortunate woman when she feels that her fate is inevitable. But this climax is prepared with the utmost care, and the audience are rather absorbed than startled. Let us add that every personage in the tale is played with a distinctness that belongs to the highest order of acting. Seldom is a Jew so well played on the stage as Fagin is represented on the platform by Mr. Dickens, and the gradual increase of his rage to frenzy as he acquaints Sikes with the transgression of Nancy is marvellous as a natural delineation of passion. To the Jew, lively in his anger, are contrasted the burglar, with his stolid brutality, and the half-knowing, half-stupid Claypole, on whose character a light is thrown by the "reading" that is scarcely to be found in the book. Though a gentleman in an ordinary evening dress is the only object presented to the spectators, the personages in the story, by the mere agency of voice and gesture, become so many separate beings, whose course is followed with rapt attention, and it is not till the reading is over that the hearers are roused from the delusion created by the reader.

from "Mr. Dickens's First Reading," *The New York Times* (10 December 1867)

Mr. Dickens gave his first reading in New York last evening at Steinway Hall. The hall was filled, of course, but, thanks to the admirable arrangements, it was not crowded nor made in the least uncomfortable by the pressure of those who were unprovided with tickets for seats. A very limited number of admissions to "standing-room only" seem to have been sold, but no more than could be properly accommodated themselves, without incommoding[1] anybody else. The audience was select, though large, and comprised a far larger proportion of professional and literary gentlemen than is usually seen at entertainments of any sort in our City.

While there is nothing in the reading to arouse noisy or demonstrative enthusiasm in an audience, there is everything to impress and delight such an audience as that assembled last evening. There are doubtless some persons living who have seen and heard Sir Walter Scott,[2] and they certainly must cherish the memory of that meeting as among the most memorable events of their lives. But it is not more noteworthy, nor will it be cherished longer or more pleasantly, than the occasion afforded last evening for the first time to see many of Mr. Dickens's hearers. Mr. Dickens is as great a genius in fiction as Sir Walter Scott; he has given as great delight to the world, and has moved far more deeply and touched more powerfully the deepest springs of emotion and affection in the human heart than even that great master of human nature and the English tongue; and he will take as high a place as he in the immortal literature of the richest language now spoken or written on the earth. To hear such a man read one of the sweetest and choicest of his own productions, will be an event in the life of any man worthy of remembrance, and it would be a tradition for descendants if the happier fortune of our day did not bring it within the personal experience of more persons than ever read or heard of Sir Walter Scott during his lifetime. It was clearly some such thought as this—thoughts of the Author and his Works as well as of the Reader and his immediate performance, that stirred the heart of

---

1 *incommoding* I.e., inconveniencing, distressing, or discomforting.
2 *Sir Walter Scott* Popular Scottish author (1771–1832) whose works include *Ivanhoe* (1819) and *Rob Roy* (1817).

last evening's audience, and prompted the hearty and prolonged applause which greeted Mr. Dickens as he walked upon the stage, with rapid stop, a calm and self-possessed air, as of one quite at home and, though a stranger, sure of a cordial welcome. Mr. Dickens is twenty-five years older than when he visited us before.[1] His appearance, of course, has changed correspondingly. He has not by any means the look of an old man, though his mustache and beard are thickly sprinkled with gray; his hair is thin and brushed forward over the crown of his head, and his general air and manner thoroughly indicated sound health and digestion, and a hale, hearty good sense and good humor. He acknowledged the applause which greeted his presence by a quiet bow, repeated once or twice as the applause continued, and then said that he was to have the pleasure of reading *A Christmas Carol*, in four parts—which he forthwith proceeded to do, announcing the title of the first part, "Marley's Ghost."

Mr. Dickens's voice is not strong, nor penetrating in the elocutionist's sense of the word. It strikes one unaccustomed to it indeed at first as a little husky; but it is distinct and sympathetic, capable of a good deal of modulation, and easily heard in every part of a larger hall than that in which he read. There is in it apparently a slight approach to a lisp—something like that peculiarity which is so marked in the voice of Reverdy Johnson.[2] Reading, indeed, is scarcely an appropriate term for his performance, which is rather a recitation, as he rarely refers to the printed page before him, and departs sometimes quite widely from its text. In the first pages of the Carol, which are merely descriptive, his "reading" was simply that and nothing more—distinguished only by admirable utterance and enunciation, and a most discriminating and effective emphasis. There was not the slightest affectation or effort at effect—very little gesticulation, and nothing to distinguish the performance from the ordinary reading of a gentleman in his parlor. But when he came to the introduction of characters and to dialogue, the reading changed to acting—and Mr. Dickens here showed a remarkable and peculiar power. Old Scrooge seemed present: every muscle of his face, and every tone of his harsh and domineering voice

---

1   *Mr. Dickens is … before* Dickens first visited America in 1842, a trip which included a month-long stay in New York City.

2   *Reverdy Johnson* Politician (1796–1876) who served as Senator for Maryland (1845–49) and Attorney General of the United States (1849–50).

revealed his character. And the effect of this admirable acting was still more marked in some of the other characters. [...]

Mr. Dickens fully proves in these readings the truth of what has often been said: that he is one of the best of living actors. The writer of this paragraph once saw him act in an amateur performance of Bulwer's "Not So Bad As We Seem,"[1] and afterward in a face of his own. In the former, which was "serious" business, he was good; but in the latter he was inimitable. He played in succession several characters—all comic, and among them his own *Sairey Gamp*—and we certainly have rarely, if ever, seen comic acting equal to it. It was easy, graceful, never overdone or overdrawn; and its effect was irresistible.

It is easy to see that very much of the effect produced upon an audience by Mr. Dickens's reading is due to *what is read*, and that it is not wholly due to his manner of reading. But this also is his own legitimate triumph, and it is one of the felicities in the fortune of those who attend these entertainments that they can hear such marvelous and wonderful productions of genius read by their author. While it gratifies a natural and rational curiosity to see the men who have made themselves immortal by the instruction and delight they have given the world, it gives us also a clearer insight into the real nature of their creations and the real meaning of the lessons they have taught mankind. We have had, and still have, in New York very many sources of intellectual and artistic amusement and delight; but we never have had, and we venture to say we never shall have, any entertainments more charming in themselves, or more full of genuine, legitimate and elevating pleasure than these readings of Mr. Dickens.

---

1 *"Not So Bad As We Seem"* Written by Edward Bulwer-Lytton (1803–73), an English writer, the play was performed in order to raise money for the Guild of Literature and Art, which Dickens and Bulwer-Lytton founded together.

Buying Tickets for the Dickens Readings at Steinway Hall, Harper's Weekly, 28 December 1867. People began lining up outside Steinway Hall late on 8 December 1867, the night before Dickens's first reading in New York. All 2,500 seats sold out.

from "Mr. Dickens as a Reader," *The New York Times* **(16 December 1867)**

Mr. Charles Dickens commences his second series of readings at Steinway Hall tonight. It is gratifying also to know that he has already announced a further series, which will commence on Monday next. [...]

It is not improper on this occasion, when the conclusions of the critic may be approved or disapproved by the coming experiences of the spectator, to dwell somewhat on Mr. Dickens's claims as a reader. There is, to be sure, a certain degree of audacity in the task. The unthinking will affirm that an author must naturally be the best exponent of his own works. To all such a sight of Mr. Dickens and the sound of his voice would, under any circumstances, be sufficient. It would be superfluous to tell them that whilst art and inspiration sometimes go together, they are very seldom found travelling in different directions, and that to recite *properly* is quite as difficult as to write well. [...]

It will suffice for our purpose to say that in the highest walks it rarely happens that a man can do two things equally well. We are of opinion that Mr. Dickens forms no exception to the rule.

And here let it be conceded at once that no one would have expected him to display this rare power had it not been so frequently dinned into our ears, that he was without an elocutionary rival, professional or otherwise. There are writers, indeed, who still persist in regarding him in this light. But it is vain to disguise that among those who, with all loyalty, assembled at Steinway Hall on the four evenings of last week, there prevails on this point a feeling of keen disappointment. Enthusiasm for the man has to a certain degree covered it up, but it has on many occasions found tolerably loud expression. It is necessary to the intercepts of art that it should be even more distinctly affirmed. No possible injury can accrue to Mr. Dickens, for were he the worst reader in the world people would still flock to his entertainments. It is only the claim that he is the best reader in the world that need be discussed, for he is very far from being the worst.

Mr. Dickens's selections are recited dramatically; that is to say, with a certain representative character in the voice and bearing. All such efforts are failures, more or less. There is a great deal of uniformity in nature, and one person who tries to imitate a dozen must necessarily diverge from and distort it. The ventriloquist, with a full range of viscera,[1] not usually devoted to conversation seldom can imitate more than two or three voices, and these in a way that is more ludicrous than entertaining. Mr. Dickens's voice is neither powerful nor flexible. It is heard to the best advantage in purely narrative passages, where a slight emphasis impresses or illumines the onward path of the story. At such moments it is singularly happy. If the emphasis be a comic one, the author gives a dry squeeze to his face and a slight vibration to the eyelid, which conveys the thought to the listener's mind in quite a button-hole-y sort of way. Every reader knows how frequent are these passages, and every auditor will agree with us that they are singularly felicitous. The slight but pleasant and conversational lisp which Mr. Dickens possesses rather assists him on those occasions. It carries out that direct man to man impression which his writings inspire, and is evidently one of those things which he neither cares to disguise nor exaggerate. Directness is the characteristic of the man, as it is of all true greatness. In this matter of the readings there is nothing superfluous. Precisely at 8 o'clock the gas is turned up and Dickens turned on. He walks rapidly to the desk; deposits there a book, which looks like a postage-stamp album; bows to the audience; looks over them for the most part, into them occasionally, but always with an eye that is remembering rather than observing; turns over a few pages of the album mechanically with his long fingers and still longer thumb, and then says in a breath, and with scarcely so much as a comma's pause: "Ladies and gentlemen, I shall have the honor of reading to you to-night the story of Little Dombey. Rich Mr. Dombey sat in the corner of his wife's darkened bed-chamber, in the great arm-chair by the bedside, and rich Mr. Dombey's son lay tucked up warm in a little basket, carefully placed on a low settee in front of the fire and close to it, as if his constitution were analogous to that of a muffin, and it was essential to toast him brown while he was very new." The reference to the muffin and the toasting is indicated to the audience, and after the flash comes the roar.[2] These hints in the narrative parts never fail. They are aimed with precision, and never miss the mark.

---

1 *viscera* Literally, bowels or "insides"; figuratively, presumably, voices.
2 *after the ... roar* Cf. Job 37.3–4.

But it becomes far more difficult to follow and sympathise with Mr. Dickens when he touches on the pathetic. It may be that the many beautiful creations of his mind have so sunk into the hearts of readers that they regard them with the fondness of parents, and consider that they are maltreated by all others whose affections are not as their own. We are certain that few would exchange their ideals of poor Bracko and Paul Dombey for the mendicant[1] varieties of those characters presented by Mr. Dickens. We are certain that the twin sufferers from the world's cruelty and arrogance, when they first came to the tender and sensitive mind of the author, did not whine there in simple monotony as they do on the platform of Steinway Hall. In other words, we are certain that Mr. Dickens, in trying to imitate the voices and manners of children and of those who are in tribulation, does injustice to himself and to the touching gracefulness with which he has written of the little ones, and of those who bear heavy burdens. There is nothing tender in his voice; nothing that wins by contrast. Little Dombey and Toots differ from each other only in being at opposite ends of the same gamut,[2] the one a shrill treble, the other a gruff bass, and, to our thinking, both mouthy and unnatural. The result of this is an air of extreme artificiality, and an impression which is repugnant to one's own sense of reading. It demands, moreover, increased artificiality in the filling up of the other parts. Where the points are so far apart, everything has to be stretched. Even Miss Blimber, with her constitutional, suffers from a pert acerbity[3] which is not indicated in the novel. [...]

It seems to us, then, that in much that is humorous, and in all that is purely narrative, interspersed with touches of humor, Mr. Dickens is excellent, and that in everything else he fails. His face is not mobile, and its expression is frequently hard. His action is purely elementary and timid; and, lastly, his power of individuality, so remarkable as a writer, is entirely subservient in his capacity as a reader. There are a dozen "poor players"[4] in the City who could read Mr. Dickens's works with better effect than their author.

---

1 *mendicant* I.e., beggarly.
2 *gamut* I.e., range of musical notes.
3 *pert acerbity* Impudence and bitterness in mannerism and speech.
4 *"poor players"* Bad actors; cf. *Macbeth* 5.5.24.

But where is another in all the wide world who could write them? And until this question can be answered from twenty million tongues Mr. Charles Dickens, read he well or read he badly, will continue to draw.[1] It may make us confused to acknowledge it, but it is the man we want to see; it would surely make us mean to say that it was his transcendent skill as an elocutionist that we principally admire. There is something very noble in being curious about great men, and something very paltry in pretending that we are not. The lecture room is nothing but a shambling remnant of a prosy past, and readings as a rule show either the disinclination or incapacity of an audience to read for itself. Mr. Dickens is of the present, and those who are frank and sincere say to themselves when they leave the hall, "I don't care a rush about his ability as a professional reader. It would be a misfortune to the world if he were a professional reader. What I wanted was to see and hear the man who has brought light and happiness to me and mine for twenty-five long years; who has kindled a brighter flame on my hearth when I have been present, and given a holier significance to it when I have been away; and who has made me not only mindful of myself but of others. A fig for everything else." And so the critics, like the malcontents, are brushed away. [...]

Mark Twain, "Charles Dickens," *The Alta California* (5 February 1868)

I only heard him read once. It was in New York, last week. I had a seat about the middle of Steinway Hall, and that was rather further away from the speaker than was pleasant or profitable.

Promptly at 8 P.M., unannounced, and without waiting for any stamping or clapping of hands to call him out, a tall, "spry," (if I may say it) thin-legged old gentleman, gotten up regardless of expense, especially as to shirt-front and diamonds, with a bright red flower in his button-hole, gray beard and moustache, bald head, and with side hair brushed fiercely and tempestuously forward, as if its owner were sweeping down before a gale of wind, the very Dickens came! He did not emerge upon the stage—that is rather too deliberate a word—he strode. He strode—in the most English way and exhibiting the most

---

1 *draw* I.e., attract listeners.

English general style and appearance—straight across the broad stage, heedless of everything, unconscious of everybody, turning neither to the right nor the left—but striding eagerly straight ahead, as if he had seen a girl he knew turn the next corner. He brought up handsomely in the centre and faced the opera glasses. His pictures are hardly handsome, and he, like everybody else, is less handsome than his pictures. That fashion he has of brushing his hair and goatee so resolutely forward gives him a comical Scotch-terrier look about the face, which is rather heightened than otherwise by his portentous dignity and gravity. But that queer old head took on a sort of beauty, bye and bye, and a fascinating interest, as I thought of the wonderful mechanism within it, the complex but exquisitely adjusted machinery that could create men and women, and put the breath of life into them and alter all their ways and actions, elevate them, degrade them, murder them, marry them, conduct them through good and evil, through joy and sorrow, on their long march from the cradle to the grave, and never lose its godship over them, never make a mistake! I almost imagined I could see the wheels and pulleys work. This was Dickens—Dickens. There was no question about that, and yet it was not right easy to realize it. Somehow this puissant[1] god seemed to be only a man, after all. How the great do tumble from their high pedestals when we see them in common human flesh, and know that they eat pork and cabbage and act like other men.

Mr. Dickens had a table to put his book on, and on it he had also a tumbler, a fancy decanter and a small bouquet. Behind him he had a huge red screen—a bulkhead—a sounding-board, I took it to be—and overhead in front was suspended a long board with reflecting lights attached to it, which threw down a glory[2] upon the gentleman, after the fashion in use in the picture-galleries for bringing out the best effects of great paintings. Style!—There is style about Dickens, and style about all his surroundings.

He read David Copperfield. He is a bad reader, in one sense—because he does not enunciate his words sharply and distinctly—he does not cut the syllables cleanly, and therefore many and many of them fell dead before they reached our part of the house. (I say "our"

---

1 *puissant* Influential.
2 *glory* Glow or halo.

because I am proud to observe that there was a beautiful young lady with me—a highly respectable young white woman.) I was a good deal disappointed in Mr. Dickens' reading—I will go further and say, a great deal disappointed. The Herald and Tribune critics must have been carried away by their imaginations when they wrote their extravagant praises of it. Mr. Dickens' reading is rather monotonous, as a general thing; his voice is husky; his pathos is only the beautiful pathos of his language—there is no heart, no feeling in it—it is glittering frostwork; his rich humor cannot fail to tickle an audience into ecstasies save when he reads to himself. And what a bright, intelligent audience he had! He ought to have made them laugh, or cry, or shout, at his own good will or pleasure—but he did not. They were very much tamer than they should have been.

He pronounced Steerforth "St'yaw-futh." This will suggest to you that he is a little Englishy in his speech. One does not notice it much, however. I took two or three notes on a card…. Every passage Mr. D. read, with the exception of those I have noted, was rendered with a degree of ability far below what his reading reputation led us to expect. I have given "first impressions." Possibly if I could hear Mr. Dickens read a few more times I might find a different style of impressions taking possession of me. But not knowing anything about that, I cannot testify.

Descriptions

The popularity of Dickens and his readings was such that several writers were inspired to publish descriptions of his performances. Of these accounts, among the most evocative are those by Kate Field and by Charles Kent.

As Mark Twain observed, around the time of the 1867 American tour the nation was "in a frenzy of enthusiasm about Dickens." Kate Field (1838–96)—an American journalist, lecturer, actor, and public personality in her own right—took advantage of the opportunity this enthusiasm afforded, enjoying considerable success with her review articles recounting his readings. This work became the basis for her *Pen Photographs of Charles Dickens*, in which she describes typical performances of each text performed during the twenty-five readings she witnessed.

Charles Dickens as a Reader is the work of Charles Kent (1832–1902), an English newspaper editor who was a close friend of Dickens and attended performances throughout the author's reading career. Although Dickens died before the book was finished, he had approved his friend's plan to write descriptions of the readings, and Kent was given access to the author's prompt copies and other materials to aid in the project.

from Kate Field, *Pen Photographs of Charles Dickens's Readings* (1868)

from David Copperfield

[...] In Micawber, Dickens undergoes as much of a transformation as if he enjoyed a patent-right to the necromancer's "Presto, change." I see him "swelling wisibly before my wery eyes,"[1] as he tips backward and forward, first on his heels and then on his toes. Before he stops swelling, he becomes just about the size of our ideal Micawber; his face, quite apoplectic in hue, is fenced in by a wall of shirt-collar; he twirls his eye-glass with peculiar grace; and when he exclaims, "My

---

1   *"swelling wisibly ... wery eyes"* Words spoken by Sam Weller in Dickens's *Pickwick Papers*.

dear Copperfield, this is *lux-u-rious*; this is a way of life which reminds me of the period when I was myself in a state of celibacy"—nearly choking himself to death before he arrives at "a state of celibacy"— the picture is complete. It is Micawber in "one of those momentous stages in the life of man," when he has "fallen back *for* a spring," and, previous to "a vigorous leap," is quite ready to fortify himself and the dearest partner of his greatness with a bachelor dinner and punch. Micawber's waiting for things to "turn up"; his eloquent tribute to "the influence of Woman in the lofty character of Wife"; his magnificent trifling with the word "*Discount*"; and the all-pervading cough, as inseparable from his speech as oxygen from air, are delectable.

Dickens could no more be Micawber without that cough than Micawber could have ever been at all without Dickens. It is the salt that gives the character savor. None but a great man misunderstood ever had such a propensity to choke. And when Mr. Micawber *does* cough, the two lapels of hair brushed above Dickens's ears, appear to be drawn by capillary attraction towards the sentiments spoken, and, waxing rampant, nod approvingly, as if to say, "Just so." Neither cough nor lapels are to be found in the text, but when did finite words ever express a man's soul? [...]

from MRS. GAMP

When Mr. Pecksniff applies himself to the knocker of Mrs. Gamp's front door in Kingsgate Street, High Holborn, and the neighborhood becomes "*alive* with female heads," Dickens's eyes are so distended at the extraordinary spectacle as to remove all doubt as to the possibility of such a commotion. When these ladies cry out with one accord, in a peculiarly anxious and feminine voice, "Knock at the winder, sir, knock at the winder. Lord bless you, don't lose no more time than you can help—knock at the winder," the evidence is conclusive. The street *is* alive with married ladies, and they cry aloud "as one man." There is the lady of measured medium voice and scrutinizing eye, who mentally sketches Mr. Pecksniff, and observes, "He's as pale as a muffin." There is the lady of nervous-sanguine temperament, who quickly retorts with a toss of the head, "so he ought to be, if he's the feelings of a man." There is the lady of a melancholy turn of mind and cast of countenance, the born victim of circumstances, who sees in Mr. Pecksniff her unrelenting Nemesis, and in a dejected but just-what-was-to-be-expected tone of voice remarks that "it always happened so with *her*." The three types of character are defined with photographic accuracy. The old motto "Life is short and Art is long" finds no exemplification in Dickens. He so fully appreciates human exigencies as, by a graphic short-hand of his own, to bring a vast deal of art within the boundaries of no time at all. Thus when Mrs. Gamp's dulcet voice is heard for the first time in answer to Mr. Pecksniff's raid upon the flower-pots, and she replies, "I'm a-comin'," Mrs. Gamp is her "indiwig'le" self. The recognition is immediate, and the applause enthusiastic. Were Dickens nothing more than a voice, this most expressive she would still live, for it is such a voice! Take a comb, cover it with tissue paper, and attempt to sing through it, and you have an admirable idea of the quality of Mrs. Gamp's vocal organ, provided you make the proper allowance for an inordinate use of snuff. [...]

No less clever is the suggestive sketch of Jonas Chuzzlewit. "There isn't any one you'd like to ask to the funeral, is there, Pecksniff?.... Because if there is, you know, *ask him*. We don't want to make a secret of it.... We'll have the doctor, Pecksniff, because he knows what was the matter with my father, and that it couldn't be helped." With nervous manner, twitching fingers, and with terror written upon his face, the bullying coward, now bullied by his own conscience, gasps rather than speaks in a hoarse voice, laying his hand to his throat as if ready to choke down tell-tale words, should any inadvertently escape his lips. [...]

from Charles Kent, *Charles Dickens as a Reader* (1872)

from SIKES AND NANCY

[...] In the powerful effect of it, the murder-scene immeasurably surpassed anything he had ever achieved before as an impersonator of his own creations. In its climax, it was as splendid a piece of tragic acting as had for many years been witnessed. [...]

Four of the imaginary beings of the novel were introduced, or, it should rather be said, were severally produced before us as actual embodiments. Occasionally, during one of the earlier scenes, it is true that the gentle voice of Rose Maylie was audible, while a few impressive words were spoken there also at intervals by Mr. Brownlow. But, otherwise, the interlocutors were four, and four only: to wit—Nancy, Bill Sikes, Morris Bolter, otherwise Noah Claypole, and the Jew Fagin. Than those same characters no four perhaps in the whole range of fiction could be more widely contrasted. Yet, widely contrasted, utterly dissimilar, though they are, in themselves, the extraordinary histrionic powers of their creator, enabled him to present them to view, with a rapidity of sequence or alternation, so astonishing in its mingled facility and precision, that the characters themselves seemed not only to be before us in the flesh, but sometimes one might almost have said were there simultaneously. Each in turn as portrayed by him—meaning portrayed by him not simply in the book but by himself in person—was in its way a finished masterpiece.

Looking at the Author as he himself embodied these creations—Fagin, the Jew, was there completely, audibly, visibly before us, by a sort of transformation ! [...] Whenever he spoke, there started before us—high-shouldered, with contracted chest, with birdlike claws, eagerly anticipating by their every movement the passionate words fiercely struggling for utterance at his lips—that most villainous old tutor of young thieves, receiver of stolen goods, and very devil incarnate: his features distorted with rage, his penthouse eyebrows (those wonderful eyebrows!) working like the antennae of some deadly reptile, his whole aspect, half-vulpine, half-vulture-like, in its hungry wickedness. [...]

As for the Author's embodiment of Sikes—the burly ruffian with thews of iron and voice of Stentor[1]—it was only necessary to hear that infuriated voice, and watch the appalling blows dealt by his imaginary bludgeon in the perpetration of the crime, to realise the force, the power, the passion, informing the creative mind of the Novelist at once in the original conception of the character, and then, so many years afterwards, in its equally astonishing representation.

It was in the portrayal of Nancy, however, that the genius of the Author-Actor found the opportunity, beyond all others, for its most signal manifestation. Only that the catastrophe was in itself, by neces-

---

1   *thews* Muscles; *Stentor* Preternaturally loud-voiced herald in Homer's *Iliad*.

sity so utterly revolting, there would have been something exquisitely pathetic in many parts of that affecting delineation. The character was revealed with perfect consistency throughout—from the scene of suppressed emotion upon the steps of London Bridge, when she is scared with the eldritch horror of her forebodings, down to her last gasping, shrieking apostrophes, to "Bill, dear Bill," when she sinks, blinded by blood, under the murderous blows dealt upon her upturned face by her brutal paramour.

Then, again, the horror experienced by the assassin afterwards! So far as it went, it was as grand a reprehension of all murderers as hand could well have penned or tongue have uttered. It had about it something of the articulation of an avenging voice not against Sikes only, but against all who ever outraged, or ever dreamt of outraging, the sanctity of human life. And it was precisely this which tended to sublimate an incident otherwise of the ghastliest horror into a homily of burning eloquence, the recollection of which among those who once saw it revealed through the lips, the eyes, the whole aspect of Charles Dickens will not easily be obliterated. [...]

What is as striking as anything in all this Reading, however—that is, in the Reading copy of it now lying before us as we write—is the mass of hints as to by-play in the stage directions for himself, so to speak, scattered up and down the margin. "Fagin raised his right hand, and shook his trembling forefinger in the air," is there, on p. 101, in print. Beside it, on the margin in MS., is the word "Action." Not a word of it was said. It was simply *done*. Again, immediately below that on the same page—Sikes' *loquitur*[1]—"'Oh! you haven't, haven't you?' passing a pistol into a more convenient pocket ['Action,' again, in MS. on the margin.] 'That's lucky for one of us—which one that is don't matter.'" Not a word was said about the pistol—the marginal direction was simply attended to. [...]

---

1   *loquitur* Latin: speaking.

CHARLES DICKENS AS HE APPEARS WHEN READING.—Sketched by C. A. Barry.—[See Page 782.]

C.A. Barry, *Charles Dickens as He Appears When Reading, Harper's Weekly*, 7 December 1867.

James Bacon, *Charles Dickens.*

from the publisher

A name never says it all, but the word "broadview" expresses a good deal of the philosophy behind our company. We are open to a broad range of academic approaches and political viewpoints. We pay attention to the broad impact book publishing and book printing has in the wider world; we began using recycled stock more than a decade ago, and for some years now we have used 100% recycled paper for most titles. As a Canadian-based company we naturally publish a number of titles with a Canadian emphasis, but our publishing program overall is internationally oriented and broad-ranging. Our individual titles often appeal to a broad readership too; many are of interest as much to general readers as to academics and students.

Founded in 1985, Broadview remains a fully independent company owned by its shareholders—not an imprint or subsidiary of a larger multinational.

If you would like to find out more about Broadview and about the books we publish, please visit us at **www.broadviewpress.com**. And if you'd like to place an order through the site, we'd like to show our appreciation by extending a special discount to you: by entering the code below you will receive a 20% discount on purchases made through the Broadview website.

Discount code: **broadview20%**

Thank you for choosing Broadview.

Please note: this offer applies only to sales of bound books within the United States or Canada.

LIST
of products used:

436 lb(s) of Rolland Enviro100 Print
100% post-consumer

RESULTS
Based on the Cascades products you selected
compared to products in the industry made with
100% virgin fiber, your savings are:

4 trees

3,607 gal. US of water
39 days of water consumption

456 lbs of waste
4 waste containers

1,185 lbs CO2
2,248 miles driven

6 MMBTU
28,110 60W light bulbs for one hour

4 lbs NOx
emissions of one truck during 5
days